TANGO – 5 (B

Survival!

by

Mitch Bouchette

This work of fiction is dedicated to Lisette, my bride of over three decades. She inspires me, motivates me, and challenges me. She gives my life real meaning.

Chapter 1: New Years Eve

"Take the shot! Damn it, take the shot!" His partner, Hansel, sounded almost like he was pleading.

But the shooter, Heinrich, ignored the man who was his fulltime partner, and sometimes friend.

Hansel tried again, "Heinrich, this is New Year's Eve. Tomorrow will be 1985! People are celebrating and there are fireworks, flashes of light and explosions everywhere. No one will see one lone muzzle flash and no one will hear the shot. It will sound like just one more of the fireworks. This is the perfect cover for a gunshot, I know it and you know it!" Hansel insisted in that irritating, whining, pleading voice that grated on Heinrich's nerves.

Heinrich always felt like he was explaining a simple concept to a child who refused to listen. He sighed audibly and said calmly, "It is not the time. The 'lady' was very specific and Alfred was very specific. And both of them said that some guy named Valdimir was also very specific."

Those were the only words the soft-spoken marksman, Heinrich, said to his more desperate, aggressive and sometimes jittery, as well as nervous, colleague. The shooter looked through his high-power scope, while the spotter saw the same scene through a pair of powerful binoculars. The two associates looked briefly at each other in silence and then back to their subjects who they were not yet cleared to engage. The target was across the ravine and slightly uphill of their location.

Not that far away, when seen through a scope, and a pair of binoculars, Charles Travis Lemon stood on the corner balcony of his villa, his home in Spain. He stood leaning casually against the wrought iron railing with his back to the Spanish Costa Brava. Travis had a glass of champagne in his hand and was raising a toast to Julie. She was the attractive and well-dressed woman who was standing to his left.

Travis thought she looked absolutely radiant in a form fitting gown and stiletto heels that were clearly not designed for walking. Well, he thought, at least they were not designed to walk very far; maybe across the bedroom later. But, what he said out loud was, "Here is to a year that I hope and pray will bring 'salud, amor, y pesetas y el tiempo para disfrutarlos,' to all of us."

It was an old, and well-known, toast for "health, love and wealth and the time to enjoy them," but it was also exactly what the assembled group expected. It was what they expected from an expat businessman who they all knew as Trav. Trav, as his friends here called him, owned and operated a small but very successful local import/export business in Alicante on the east coast of Spain.

Trav and Julie were considered by all who knew them to be the perfect couple; he was fit and trim and in very good physical shape. And Julie, who worked with the airlines, was outgoing, friendly and an absolute knockout to look upon. She looked especially great this evening; but ironically, on a day-to-day basis, she intentionally toned down certain aspects of her physical appearance. When she went to the office at the airline, she saw no point in attracting excessive attention from the average Iberian male of this resort area. And she saw no reason to incite jealousy or resentment from her female co-workers who might not be quite as striking as she was.

The remainder of the group at the house for this New Year celebration were business associates. They came mostly from the local area and from some of the surrounding towns and villages. As the clock moved relentlessly toward midnight the serving staff came out with the traditional twelve grapes for each guest. The long ago established custom was to eat one grape with each stroke of the clock as it rang in the New Year.

Thus with the traditional Spanish toast and the obligatory sip of champagne done, what followed was an equally traditional kiss and a hug with one's partner. But the toast was not considered over until hugs, and some polite kisses, as well as manly back slapping and smiles were exchanged with the other guests in the room. Then, as if on some sort of silent cue, the men began to gravitate towards the bar in the corner of the large balcony.

The view from the balcony, over the shoreline, with the moon and stars reflecting in the water, was one of a kind. And, of course there were the staccato interruptions of fireworks and lights all along The Costa Brava. It was an impressive and festive view that this group of friends was enjoying this New Year's Eve

And as if on that same silent cue, the women seemed to float a little further into the villa and out of the night air. They settled into a sitting area inside the home and all the while the conversation never missed a beat. In fact it didn't even pause; and there was no break to the pleasant cheerful sounds. It was in fact a lively, animated discussion among friends in both locations.

"You know, gentlemen, it is interesting to me and perhaps even funny how the men eventually wind up in one place. And of course the women always seem to gather in another, different place." Travis noted, and then added, "But, I guarantee you that if we had started the evening by asking all the women to sit in there and all the men to come out here . . ." But he never got to finish the remark.

"It would have been an argument for sure, and maybe a real fight!" Diego Rivera, a local vintner, declared.

"No, no my friend, you soft pedal the issue, it would not have been a fight, it would have been a declaration of war. And win, lose or draw, everyone of us would be ending the evening sleeping on the sofa in our front rooms!" Raul Osborne interjected and the group smiled knowingly.

"Hey, don't underestimate the dynamics, Raul," Trav added, "The night is young and some of us could wind up there still." Then changing the subject slightly, "Forgive me a moment, but on that note, I am leaving you all and going to check that the ladies have what they want to drink. Please, gentlemen, serve yourselves and refresh your own drinks from the bar here." Trav indicated a well stocked burled wood bar on the edge of the balcony.

Julie smiled up at Travis from where she sat perched on a high backed armchair in the center of the cluster of ladies. "Oh, darling, are you here to take our drink orders?"

Wow, the estrogen is so thick in here you could cut it with a knife was what Trav thought but what he said was, "Absolutely! Starting with the most beautiful woman in the room, what would you like Julie?"

And then he pretended to ignore the smiles of the other wives and girlfriends as he kept his gaze on Julie. She blushed ever so slightly and said, "Perhaps some more of this wine that Diego brought." Then shifting immediately to Gretschen, Diego Rivera's German born wife, Julie added, "Gretschen, would you like some of Diego's special wine also?"

Gretschen cleared her throat and said, "Well it is New Year's, so at the risk of scandalizing you ladies, what I would like is a nice cold beer. I am after all a German and we get plenty of wine at my house!" Gretschen added with a mischievous smile and there were appreciative twitters of polite laughter.

"Gretschen," Amalia spoke up, "you know that Travis is going to tell Diego! But before he does that, Trav dear boy, could I have another glass of that delightful champagne we are sipping." Then in an aside to the group, "With Raul so focused on his fighting bulls, I have had enough beef and red wine for a while."

A few moments later Travis had the drink orders and the group was already absorbed in conversation about fashion and the new music coming from overseas. The fashion they were discussing of course meant Paris and Milan, not Los Angeles or New York; but the music meant the US.

Even as he left the room, he noted that the women were acting as though he had never even been there. The thought occurred to him that this was a little like walking across the shallow end of a swimming pool and then looking back to try and see your footsteps. These people all knew each other well socially and were all clearly very comfortable with each other. That was clear from the body language.

As he returned to the balcony and made his way to the bar to serve the ladies' orders, he noticed that his new bottle of single malt whisky had taken a hit and made a note to bring another one from storage later. "Coming through," Travis said, "man on a mission!"

Back With Heinrich And Hansel

The watchers, Heinrich the shooter and Hansel the spotter, saw all the movements on the balcony. Of course they watched them through the crosshairs of a riflescope and the range markers of a pair of binoculars; even if they could not hear the dialogue. "I am telling you, Heinrich, to go ahead and take the shot! Tomorrow you will regret not taking the shot!"

But this time the shooter just looked over at his associate and then looked back to the riflescope. "And, Hansel, if I do not follow orders, from the lady, there will be hell to pay! Do you not know this action goes past even Alfred, and all the way to Dresden, and who knows where beyond that!" That was what he wanted to say, to remind his spotter why they were there in the first place; but he kept his silence.

At The New Year's Eve Party

Back at the house on the luxuriously appointed balcony that was partially outdoors and partially indoors, Raul interjected, "Gino. Let Trav in there

11

beside you and give him a hand. It is in all our best interests to keep the ladies happy or two things will happen. First we will never get a chance to discuss sports, politics and banking." The group smiled and Raul continued, "And, secondly he will face a fate worse than one of my fighting bulls when he is being attacked in the bull ring."

With that the group stifled a laugh and Gino interjected in a quiet voice, "You know, Raul is right! Here, Trav, let me help you out. I will help you serve them as well. You can trust me, I have experience from my hotels in keeping the guests happy."

Gino and Travis made short work of delivering the dinks and then retreating as Julie nodded a thank you at Trav and Anita, Gino's fiancé, smiled at him and winked. As they retreated to the balcony, the conversation was just warming up. "Trav," Diego said, "you're in the import and export business, what do you think?"

"Gino and Trav looked at each other and it was obvious that he had missed something. Travis replied, "What do I think about what? That you gentlemen

12

have extraordinary taste in women?" Travis said by way of deflecting and then added, "Though looking around here I suspect the ladies themselves may all be in need of eye glasses."

"OK mister wise guy, have your joke!" Diego replied, "The question was about the rumors of a personal computer coming for sale very soon. Is there a market for such a thing? What are you hearing?"

Travis Lemon the businessman was being asked a question. But Travis Lemon the covert operative, who had just finished a refresher at the facility in Langley, Virginia last month, knew a lot more than they did about the topic. In fact he knew a lot more than he could share with his friends. Sometime early in the next year, probably January or February, a so-called personal computer would be marketed and this would make his life a lot easier. At least that was the belief among the technical people back at Langley. They felt it would in fact be some sort of a "game changer."

Travis had been convinced and decided he would use his business access to pull a couple of the first available from a shipment. He planned to keep one for the office and one for his home. Publically, he would justify it all as "for business purposes." That is how he would cover the fact that he already had one in his home office and he was using it to communicate with his "Boss in Madrid" with an encryption device and a modem that could call an unlisted private phone number and synchronize information.

"Well," Trav began, "I read in a trade journal that the Apple Macintosh is due within a couple of months. And, I hear that it is likely to cost around two thousand five hundred US dollars, give or take a little bit." Trav kept his comments to a minimum. "But I have no idea what the capacity or speed of the processor will be like." Then he added, "Why, what have you guys heard?"

Diego responded, "Well I started this particular topic because I really could use something that can help me with inventory control. All that wine I make does not sort itself and I need a solution that doesn't cost an arm and a leg in accountant salaries to get it done right. Besides, dealing with IBM is a giant pain in the butt." Then he paused to take a sip of his whiskey.

Raul picked up the thread, "Yeah, tell me about it. They only got like one big solution, and man it is expensive! It is like an electronic spreadsheet but they try to make that one solution fit every local business problem. For me, counting bulls and cows is easy, even the workers can handle that part most of the time."

That got a little chuckle from the group, and he continued, "But if I want to track the feed, nutrients, weight gain, etc., etc., then they gonna' try to sell me the same stuff Gino uses for tracking his guests and Diego uses to count bottles of wine. By the way, amigo, I would be glad to come count your wine myself anytime. And you can pay me in wine!" That also got a laugh from the whole group.

"Tell me, Trav, you follow politics in America?" Raul asked during a lull in the conversation.

"Yes, but only sometimes. Why?" Travis responded smiling.

"Just thinking; you guys elected an actor for President and so far he has put a woman on the Supreme Court, back a few years ago with Sandra Day

Oconnor. And this past year he sent a woman into space. You know the one I mean, Sally Ride, the astronaut. Then when a little island coup started and the rebels refused to guarantee the safety of American citizens, he sent the military to invade Grenada."

Everyone was nodding as Raul continued, "That is all looking pretty good to most Spanish business people. Besides over here on the Iberian Peninsula, all we got now is a bunch of Socialists after our last election. And they want to vote on getting out of NATO! How can we be so far out of step with the US?"

Gino jumped in, "Maybe you should declared war on the US and then surrender immediately and ask for reconstruction 'after the war.' It seemed to work for Italy!" Diego almost sprayed his drink across the room laughing.

Julie chose that moment to come out onto the patio, "What are you gentlemen discussing and what is so funny?"

Raul answered first, "Oh, Gino was telling us his plan to run for politics and what his plan of action might be."

Julie looked to Travis for some clue of what was going on and he returned her gaze smiling warmly into her eyes. Then he said, "Have we been neglecting the ladies? Do we need to freshen up their drinks?"

"Yes, that would be a good idea." Julie said smiling that five hundred watt smile that always warmed him. "And, I will go tell Anita about Gino's political aspirations."

As she turned to leave the group, Trav saw the conspiratorial look in her eye and added, "Gino and I will be right in. I can't wait to see what Anita has to say about becoming a public wife as 'Mrs. Politico'!"

Everyone was smiling except Gino who was already busy at the bar setting up glasses and some ice. Under his breath he complained, "Minding my own business, quietly enjoying my drink, and you guys still manage to set me up. Just wait until you want to reserve a room for a visitor or want a reservation in the dining room. You do know we keep a list of people to watch, don't you?" The evening continued in a good-natured way until the wee hours of the morning. To say they all enjoyed each other's company would be an understatement. This collection of friends got along extremely well!

New Year's Day

The next morning Travis rose early and made a cup of coffee; then he retired to his home office and booted up the square machine on his desk and connected with his Boss in Madrid. He paused with the coffee in mid air as he read the screen. Tango Alpha was directing him, Tango Section operative number 5, to head to Turkey with all haste. His in-place requirement was in two days.

No problem, he thought, he would spend New Year's Day with Julie and then leave the day after on a direct hop to Istanbul. But he knew Julie would not be happy and he also knew there must be something "hot" going on for this kind of unexpected trip on such short notice. He knew he would find out all the details soon enough as he shut the machine down and secured the line.

Chapter 2: Alfred In The Frankfurt Office

Alfred sat, exhaled and opened the top right hand drawer of the desk that had once belonged to Sergei. Sergei Ivanovich, his old boss, who had been the former cultural attaché from Moscow. He reached in and brought out the small jar of American instant coffee and sighed again. There were only two of the little jars left unopened, and after that he would have to find a way to get more of these things.

It had not taken him long to begin to understand and appreciate these little simple pleasures. That appreciation came with only a few days in Sergei's old chair at Sergei's old desk. It had been about the first week after Sergei had returned to Moscow when that arrogant bastard had called him from Dresden, East Germany.

Vladimir Vladmiravich Putin had let him know, in no uncertain terms, that he was being "watched." In other words the Dresden Office was "keeping an eye on him" and "they" expected to have a major input into what he did here in Frankfurt. And he knew that "they" were the new Stasi which was really Putin and his people.

"Well screw you Vladimir!" Alfred said under his breath, "This is not Dresden, GDR under Soviet control. This is a diplomatic mission to the FRG for Russia which is located in Frankfurt, not in Dresden. This is West Germany; this is not East Germany! We work for Moscow, and right now Moscow is too busy trying to consolidate things back home to even care."

Alfred took a breath and calmed his nerves before he spoke to his coffee cup again. "Who does he think he is anyway? He might be 'disappearing people' in Dresden, but here in Frankfurt I am in charge. Frankfurt is in the first world; it is not a third string East German city like Dresden."

Alfred did however wonder exactly what Putin knew about his role in Sergei's fall from power. And more importantly, he wondered exactly what Vladimir knew about Sergei's unfortunate fatal auto accident back in Russia. No, Alfred reasoned with himself, the man could not "know" anything; Alfred had chosen his "assassin" very carefully.

The man in Moscow was a good mechanic and well known and would never be suspected. He, Putin, could not "know" anything. Still he was an old KGB guy, just as Sergei had been; everyone knew that to such men there were no accidents in life. Still, he could not "know" anything; so again, "Screw you Vladimir!" Alfred said aloud to his coffee cup.

The cup, of course, made no response; it just sat there holding the hot dark liquid that Alfred had come to enjoy. It had always irritated him that the American military who were stationed in Germany, could just walk into their government commissaries and use their ration cards to buy whatever they wanted. These ration cards only existed as one of the last vestiges of WWII. But coffee was still on the controlled list in the FRG, The Federal Republic of Germany. The controlled list included automobile gasoline, coffee and cigarettes, oh yes and booze. One could not forget about liquor that was always on the list.

It was a kind of open secret that some of these American families used their rations to make payment for a portion of their rent with local landlords. These contraband items were in high demand with local German home owners who rented houses or apartments to the Americans. Or if the landlords were lucky enough to own rental homes near one of the American Kasernes, they might have a family member working on the Airbase or on the local US Army Post. These people then had their own little black-market smuggling operations for such luxuries. He really must figure out exactly who Sergei had been using to bring these luxuries to himself.

It was, after all, only fair since he had replaced Sergei and now occupied his old office and even his old chair. It had been some months now since Alfred had been able to engineer his superior's fall from grace, so to speak, among his boss' old boy friends inside the KGB. And of course he, Alfred, had positioned himself as the only likely successor to Comrade Sergei Ivanovich.

He had even had a plaque made in honor of his ex-supervisor and placed it on the wall in the outer office. It was displayed there now, just in case one of Sergei's old friends happened to come by. That way there could be no question about his respect for the system, and the "old guys" who were slowly being weeded out of the "new" Russian system.

But the real prize had been the small book of passwords that fit so easily into the inside coat pocket of a man's suit coat. Alfred had found it in the same drawer with the coffee and the carton of cigarettes. Sergei only smoked occasionally and Alfred did not smoke at all. But he kept the boxes of cigarettes because they were Marlboro, in those stiff little cardboard boxes with the flip tops, and they had utility. These little boxes made great small bribes and small gifts in a world where a small favor was a currency unto itself.

The American cigarettes never ceased to impress, and it was handy to have them around especially when the Iranians or the Arabs came by to talk. One of these Persian fellows came by at least twice a year, and more often most years. His name was Farouq and he was from Iran. He had apparently been trained and educated at a school in Russia where his best friend and classmate had been the son of Sergei Ivanovich, named Nikolai. So in a way this Iranian fellow, Farouq, was also a legacy from Sergei that now fell to him. But Alfred had bigger plans for Farouq than Sergei could have imagined; at least he did if he could find a way to keep Vladimir out of his business.

Nikolai, Sergei's son, everyone knew, had been killed by Charles Travis Lemon in El Salvador several years ago. That incident had driven Sergei to spend Russia's critical, and limited, resources to try to kill Lemon. Eventually that fixation for revenge had led to his removal from office, and ultimately to a "most unfortunate" and fatal accident. The brakes had "failed" on his old car just when it became clear that his misappropriation of resources in a personal vendetta for Travis Lemon, was all about to blow up in his face. But it never became public and so there was no embarrassment to the senior members of the FSB, which had mostly replaced the dreaded KGB and absorbed many of the old KGB members.

The man Farouq had risen steadily within the ranks of the IRGC, the Revolutionary Guards Corps, in Iran. He had also continued to make trips each year to check on his sister and her family here in the Federal Republic of Germany. Sergei had used Farouq at least once before in an attempt to kill Lemon but Sergei did not think big enough! He had never developed a grand design, but of course Sergei had been tied up with the personal revenge for which he lived. Alfred on the other hand saw a bigger picture and did not get so personally involved.

In fact he had just had a chat with Farouq today, and Farouq had promised Alfred that he would have a talk with some members of the PJAK. This was a Kurdish organization that was in its infancy as an idea among students inside Iran. These young Kurds in Iran had linkage to the PKK in Turkey and to the group in Syria and even into Iraq.

And this same group of the PKK were even now involved with orchestrating a masterful attempt to kill

Lemon, while making it all look like a domestic terrorist attack from inside Turkey. Alfred so hoped this one would not fail because it would go a long way to hush Putin's criticism.

He had already had some success a few days ago against two more US operatives; and those had both been successful. And Alfred's superiors in Moscow had noticed the success in a good way. Take that Putin! And they had congratulated him and encouraged him to continue to rid the world of as many of the members of Tango Section as he could find, especially if it could be made to look like someone else had done it.

Alfred would of course do exactly that, but first things first. He had to find a way to get gas coupons, instant coffee, good American whiskey and American cigarettes. He was fed up with Russian Vodka! Oh, it was good vodka but it was boring, and he wanted something a bit different and a bit better. He also wanted to make this his own personal way of thumbing his nose at the great American government. The great American government was sucking all the oxygen out of the space in Europe and it needed to be reigned in.

What was it his Brit friend had said, that the problem with Americans is they were over-fed, over-paid, over-sexed, and over here! Yes, that was it, and it was funny, and it was true. Alfred smiled to himself as he made his afternoon coffee and sat back down at the desk to enjoy it. He was thinking the whole time, "Take that Putin! I bet you are still drinking that crap East German or the low grade Turkish coffee! Enjoy Dresden you asshole!" Then Alfred rang for his assistant.

Svetlana

The young Russian woman came into his office, "You called Comrade?" she said with the hint of a smile. She was in her late twenties with a shapely figure, that she kept toned with daily exercise, and she wore the prescribed Russian clothes expected of office staff. But he noticed there was a decided western flair to her look. Perhaps, he thought, she has found a good German tailor to modify her clothes. Or perhaps she is just so good looking that even Russian clothing cannot hide her appeal.

"Yes, Svetlana, I have a task for you." Alfred said, and the added, "You have competed the technical school in Russia, have you not?"

"Yes, Comrade, I have competed the school but this is my first time out into the West. What is it you want me to do?"

Alfred liked this girl's attitude and he smiled as he said, "I want you to find us a conduit for everything on the American Ration Cards. I mean gasoline coupons, cigarettes, whiskey, coffee, everything. But," he emphasized before she could say this was beneath her training and skill level he added with emphasis, "this is only a test. You must do this by recruiting your own network, of one or of many I do not care. But it should be 'layered' so as to remove any connection to the office and it should be insulated from you personally."

"Are there any guidelines or restrictions?" Svetlana asked looking him in the eye.

"No. I don't care if you use bribery, blackmail, a honey trap, or any other method you can devise. But I caution that you should take this seriously and not treat it as a game. You see, if it fails and you are arrested for black market activities, from the official view, you were just a young woman who was stupid and corrupted by the Western decadence. You can be removed from your position and returned to Russia. And only a simple apology to the German officials will suffice to end the affair from the perspective of the office here." Alfred spelled it out bluntly and clearly for her.

Then he made a promise as well, "On the other hand if you can deliver the items on a recurring basis within a month, and do so for the next several months, then we can report this as a successful training technique to our superiors in Moscow. And you can take credit for the design of the thing."

Now Svetlana began to smile. Alfred noticed how her eyes sparkled and he realized he might be seeing her really smile for the first time. Clearly she had grasped the scope of what he was proposing. The risks were mere embarrassment for her personally, but the opportunity for the rewards were exceptional.

She said only, "I am very interested in this idea. Is there anything else, Comrade?"

"Yes, just a word of advice, this is the real world and things are not exactly like what they teach in the technical schools. So be very careful and check all the details yourself if at all possible." Alfred added as a caution because he liked this young woman. And that smile of hers, at that moment, told him that the same things motivating him motivated her.

"I will not let you down, Comrade." Svetlana said evenly.

"And, that, my dear protégé is lesson one. You do this for yourself. Do not let yourself down. This is only a small black-market operation like a dozen others that run everyday. But it is also your chance to test your skills at recruitment, planning and execution of a plan that only you designed and in which you have have confidence." Alfred added, "And if you are successful then we can also enjoy a good cup of coffee here in the office." Then Alfred gave her a smile as encouragement.

"Thank you, Comrade." Svetlana said and added, "I shall not disappoint you and I will not let myself down." She emphasized the word "myself" and Alfred smiled. Then she added, "Is there anything else for today?"

"No. You are free to go and do whatever it is young people do here in West Germany. And I shall go and do what we old people do here in West Germany. I will see you tomorrow."

Svetlana nodded curtly and turned to walk out of his office as his gaze lingered on her backside. Yes, he thought, she definitely had her own tailor here. Alfred smiled to himself as he looked off into space a moment. He was having a good day. Farouq could be used repeatedly to pressure the Iranian Kurdish students to do his bidding with the PKK in Turkey. Svetlana was going to stay out of his hair for a while and maybe get herself noticed by their superiors in Moscow. And, he would soon have more of the American coffee he enjoyed so much. Yes this was turning out to be a good day for Alfred Jakovich. So screw you Vladimir and screw Dresden too!

Sonja

But Alfred did not go home, or to his favorite bar for a drink after work. Alfred went to meet a lady at a coffee shop hidden away in a working class neighborhood. The lady was waiting when he arrived. Clearly she had once been strikingly beautiful once upon a time, but now she looked tired and a bit gaunt. In fact she looked like a recovering addict, which is exactly what she was.

Alfred stopped in front of the table and said, "Good evening, my dear, how was it today?"

"Better than yesterday." She said and motioned for him to sit. "I only had to use the substitute medication twice today and I was able to walk a bit. I even ate a nice salad." She added.

Alfred took her hand across the table and looked into her slightly bloodshot eyes with the hint of dark circles around them, that the makeup did not quite conceal, and he lied. "Sonja, you are as beautiful as ever. And the doctors of Mother Russia will help you back to control of your life." He patted her hand and added, "Even now your help and assistance is invaluable! We have taken two operatives out of this world and tomorrow we will take the man, who did this to you, out as well."

"Travis Lemon must die!" Sonja interjected, "He is the reason the Americans used the drugs to interrogate me that left me addicted and wrecked my life. You know they were supposed to kill the three of us, Heinrich, Hansel, and me. But they used the drugs on me and they beat Heinrich, but I still think Hansel told them something useful because he had the easiest time of it and then they let us live, if you can call this living!"

"I know. I know." Alfred said still patting her hand.

"But," she added, I put the sniper team in place as you suggested even though they likely will not be needed. But if Lemon survives tomorrow's action in Istanbul, then he will have a surprise when he returns home." They sat in silence a moment sharing a small pot of weak coffee. Each had his, or her, own thoughts and they smiled at each other occasionally. Finally when the coffee was gone, Alfred called the waiter over to give her a fresh pot and ordered a sandwich for each of them. They ate together then he left her to her thoughts.

Chapter 3: Hagia Sophia, Istanbul (1985)

It was a New Year and only a few days after the New Years Eve celebration on the Spanish Costa Brava. Clearly he missed being with Julie at his home in Spain; but Charles Travis Lemon had been directed to Istanbul to "fix a problem." That was, after all, what he did as one of a limited number of operatives assigned to an obscure office known as Tango Section. The operatives of this office were sent out, or "dispatched," to work specific high interest, and high threat, cases any way they could.

And that is why Travis was in Istanbul, taking in an early morning view of the Hagia Sophia. He looked like any other tourist as he waited for his morning meeting to get a "situation brief" with details of his next mission. He was enjoying the morning sunlight playing off of the curved domes of this massive and impressive, historic structure. Yes, he missed Julie and his home but he did enjoy this view and he thoroughly enjoyed this building.

In fact he made a point of finding the time to explore and admire its view every time he came to Istanbul. Of course he had long ago mastered the art of strolling along, as if he had not a care in the world, while making mental notes on every detail of the things happening around him. He was also constantly analyzing the information he passively gathered. And subconsciously, he was also comparing and connecting it with data already in his encyclopedic memory.

Details

He knew for example that in terms of population, Istanbul surpassed New York City, Paris or Rome in sheer numbers of people. And he knew it rivaled these cities in terms of international importance as a center of politics, wealth and power. "And it all goes back to a little boy from the Balkans," he said to no one. "It is truly amazing what one man can do if he puts his mind to it, and has a plan, and maybe doesn't mind changing his name once or twice."

That little boy he was thinking about had been born Petrus Sabbatius in 483 AD in Tauresium,

Dardania which is thought to be modern day Skopje, Macedonia. That part of course may be a little fuzzy depending on which historian you read. But the academic community is pretty well agreed that he died on the 14th of November in 565 AD in Constantinople. Constantinople of course is known today as Istanbul, and the little boy named Petrus is also known as Flavius Justinianus, or if you prefer Justinian I, Emperor.

Petrus was first noticed, and rapidly became known, for his brilliant administrative and organizational expertise. In a time before computers and desk calculators he made a career off the ability to see the patterns in chaos. He was a master at public government and he left the world with the Code of Justinian, or Codex Justinianus, in around 534 AD. And he undoubtedly had a first class education, although some of his contemporaries complained he spoke Greek with a bad accent, but they were probably just jealous.

Perhaps more than anything else, what Justinian is remembered for is the Hagia Sophia, which is today known in Turkey as the Holy Grand Mosque. Of course the original building was commissioned by Justinian I, then designed and built by Isidore of Miletus and Arthemius of Tralles, as a magnificent Christian Cathedral. It was built in 537 AD and was originally known as the Patriarchal Cathedral of the Imperial Capital of Constantinople. At the time it also had the distinction of being the largest Christian Church in the world.

It served first as an Eastern Orthodox Church until around 1204 AD when it became the city's Latin Catholic Cathedral for the next sixty years or so. But in 1453 AD, with the expansion of the Ottoman Empire into the area and the fall of Constantinople, it was as they say, "repurposed" as a mosque. Then in 1935 it was repurposed again by the secular Turkish Government as a museum. And by 2020 AD it would be re-opened again as a mosque but that particular fact is well after our little story when it was still serving as a museum.

So Charles Travis Lemon had once again taken on the persona of Harrison Travis Melon, who was enjoying a little cultural tour around the Hagia Museum. When his contact came into view he had to smile because it was a perfect cover. The two of them would attract no attention whatsoever in this mixed group of Christian and Muslim tourists. It seemed the building continues to attract both groups in fairly significant numbers and from all nationalities, none of that surprised him.

The thing that Trav was not expecting was this short, and very pretty, thirty-something woman who came up to him like an old friend, or maybe even an old lover. She was a little too loud which fit with the European opinion and expectation of American tourists. She put her small, gloved hands on his biceps and leaned in on tiptoes to give him a peck on the cheek.

"I am so sorry to be late, darling. I really must remember to wind my watch in the morning. Can you forgive me for being forgetful and for being just the teeniest bit late?" Sheila Makinley gushed at Harry Melon. She was wearing a very fashionable black dress with white polka' dots and a large red belt that matched her red hat and red heels.

Lemon recovered quickly in his Harry Melon persona, "Darling, a gentleman never keeps a lady waiting and he never, never notices if she is just a bit tardy. So, of course there is nothing to forgive. You are here now, so let's take our time and enjoy this beautiful building." He offered his arm and she wrapped her arm in his and rested her hand on his forearm. They walked along at an unhurried pace and chatted quietly like any other couple who might be sightseeing in Istanbul.

What no one else could hear was Harry asking, "What happened?"

"Things have really gone to shit." Sheila said with a smile on her face. "Tango Three and Tango Six are dead." That hit Travis hard but he showed no visible reaction. And he understood immediately why Sheila was back out "in the field." While he processed this news she continued, "Nobody is sure yet exactly how they were identified and targeted." Sheila, with whom he had worked closely on assignment a few years ago, back in El Salvador, was now a special assistant to Tango Alpha. The designation "Tango Alpha" was the designation for their mutual boss and the agency Head for Strategic Operations. He was also affectionately known as "the old man" but not to his face and not within his hearing.

Tango Section had always been a secretive, little known and intentionally obscure organization; and they liked it that way! It was an agency that took on the dirty work of the really tough, sticky problems. He was supposedly here to meet a lower level functionary who would just pass a package of data to him. Admittedly, Sheila had stayed on an administrative track after their time together in Central America, but she had excellent field credibility too. The fact that she had come personally to deliver a message was overkill in a big way; and it was a signal in and of itself that something was terribly wrong.

"Instructions?" Harry asked.

"Yes, find whoever is killing our operatives and stop them, anyway you can. There is a car waiting outside where we can talk more openly and I can share with you what little we know. But, after that Trav, as always you are on your own, my friend." Then in a slightly louder voice, "We really must come back here when there is more time to take in this whole marvelous place."

The two of them made small talk as she guided him with slight pressures on his arm out the door and through the well-manicured garden outside a side entrance. There, maybe fifty yards away was a waiting sedan at the edge of the property. Trav knew this is where they were heading because the car had that sort of look about it.

For starters, it was a late model vehicle and it was all black. And the passenger compartment had blacked out windows. And in Turkey only "official" cars were all black. And in case someone missed it, the blacked out passenger windows was like waving a red flag in front of a bull.

Waving a flag! A little too obvious! "Lord help me!" he thought, "This is not going to end well!" Two of his colleagues were dead and his task was to find out who and why and stop them. Trav pulled against her arm ever so slightly and Sheila looked up inquiringly.

"Can't we just talk here? There is no one around." Trav asked in a quiet voice.

"Trav, I want to show you what we have so far, including pictures, and it is all safe and sound in my little rolling, secure office, away from prying eyes and the accidental eavesdropper." Sheila emphasized the word "secure" and kept smiling the whole while, just in case someone was watching them.

"Sheila, this just does not feel right."

They were about half way to the car when the fireball ignited. First, it swallowed the car in flames. And in nearly the same instant, it sent the car flying into the air. The burning twisted hunk of metal came back down to earth about twenty yards away. Luckily it had flown in the other direction.

Then as his mind kicked into overdrive he realized, "Of course it went the other way!" Melon realized in an instant that the PKK would not want to anger the Muslin Leadership in Istanbul by dumping the burning wreck on the grounds of the revered Hagia

Sophia. The bomb had been placed so as to totally destroy the vehicle and to blow the wreckage in the other direction. It was downright "artful."

Trav was on his feet and pulling Sheila behind him, "Move he said with firm determination." All the while he was pulling her arm. She was dazed but recovering quickly. Sheila stepped out of her shoes and matched his pace in a barefooted state across the distance, and back to the entrance where they might find a degree of safety. Trav heard a few random shots and immediately assessed this as likely from a concealed shooter intended to create maximum terror and chaos. But he knew in his gut that the shooter was only a distraction. The distraction was intended to draw attention away from the real target, them!

And now Sheila and he were back inside the ancient building. They were relatively safe behind the guards of the place and catching their breath. He looked over and saw that her hat was gone and her hair was more than a little disheveled. Her dress was torn and dirty and her feet were bloody and cut.

Sheila, though was a true professional and she was calm again as she looked up at Trav and said, "Those were some of my favorite shoes, damn it! Trav, when you get these bastards, I want to have a talk with them about how hard it is to find good shoes! This is exactly why I transferred from field work to admin and research."

Melon almost laughed and he knew she could see the smile in the corners of his mouth. "Don't you dare laugh!" Sheila said trying to look stern.

"Besides the shoes and clothes though, you OK here?" Trav asked Sheila, while suppressing a smile despite the events of recent moments.

"Yeah, I'm good." Sheila replied sounding almost resigned to it all, "I just have to wait for a pickup team. You just go do what it is you do."

Travis looked her in the eye briefly, then he turned and strolled away into the mass of confused and terrified onlookers. A moment later as she looked around, he was just gone. And Sheila was being approached by an older man who made his way to her. The old man wore a shocked expression and put an arm around her shoulder as he might to a daughter. Together they started walking and went through the confusion straight to a waiting ambulance. The vehicle left as soon as they were on board.

Sheila and her pickup team made their way back to a private airstrip and she boarded a small private jet for transit back to Madrid. When they arrived, she headed directly to the Field Head Quarters for Tango Section, which operated out of the US Embassy in Madrid. She barely had time to change clothes before they were landing and she was on her way back to the Embassy to check in with Tango Alpha.

Travis Becomes Harrison Travis Melon (Again)

Harrison Travis Melon was sitting quietly at a nondescript local café down an unimportant street in a suburb of Istanbul. He was sorting his thoughts and projecting the outward demeanor, to anyone who might be observing, of a middle-aged businessman. Harry Melon looked preoccupied with his personal problems and he did not betray the gymnastics his mind was doing. He sipped his coffee and mentally ran through a checklist of all the known bad actors in the area. Then he ordered another water with lemon and another small coffee and started all over again running all the details he had through his previously noted encyclopedic and impressive memory.

He was searching for a connection, a thread, anything! There was always "something" so he must be missing "the something" and he knew it. He was resisting that fact that his mind, and therefore his subconscious, kept circling back to the Persians.

Maybe it was just the lingering influence of the Hagia Sophia on his subconscious. Or for that matter maybe it was his fixation on the problems that Justinian had with the Persians. But by the time his third cup arrived, he had come to a conclusion, at least as a place to start. His working hypothesis would be that he needed to start with the "Persians," not the Iranians but with the Kurds who came from Iran.

It was all about motive and opportunity. They would have the contacts and were the most likely conduit for a "contract job" that served Kurdish interests. For them it was even better if it came at the expense of a little terror in Turkey's leading city. And, it was better still if it served as a demonstration that they absolutely respected the Muslim Leadership even as they took out the target they were being contracted for. It also meant there might be a leak, or an informant, somewhere on the inside with access to too much information about Tango Section. That part would be Sheila's problem, he was on his way to meet some Kurds.

Chapter 4: Kurds! Kurds?

"Kurds! Kurds? Really?" The senior analyst in the intelligence fusion center, Robert "Bob" Wallis, was almost yelling. His consternation was aimed at Sheila Makinley, who had just finished relaying the outline of Trav's gut instincts. Bob was an old school analytical type who demanded two or three sources to verify everything. And Sheila was wearing soft socks and house slippers in the office as her feet healed. The doctor's orders for her footwear had not left her in a good mood and Bob was being Bob this morning. To say things between them were tense would have been an understatement!

They were in a room of sorts, specifically designed for such discussions. Well, it was not exactly designed for yelling; but it was a facility that had all kinds of protections to prevent eavesdropping of any kind. This is where the most sensitive information could be discussed without danger of compromising sources or methods, or the data itself for that matter. In other words, the kind of information that gets people killed if it becomes widely known by the adversary.

This particular room was deep in the bowels of the US Embassy in Madrid but it could have been anywhere. In another era the US spent a fortune to construct these places around the world especially in embassies and on military facilities. And the Head of Tango Section was seated at the head of the table with his executive assistant, Sheila Makinley to his right. And glaring across the table at her was the Chief of Intelligence Bob Wallis.

"Sir," Robert said looking at Tango Alpha, "I don't see it. We have nothing in SIGINT or for that matter HUMINT that indicates the PKK has a reason to want to blow up our vehicle in broad daylight, in Istanbul, in front of a national landmark like the Hagia Sophia."

Sheila did not let that pass, "Bob, you are distorting my words and that is not what I said. And, frankly, I trust Travis Lemon's gut more than I do your fancy electronic Signals Intelligence." She hated the Intelligence world's acronyms like SIGINT for Signals and HUMINT for people, why couldn't they just say that a person told them something important, or that they had heard it over their listening equipment? Why did they feel the need to obscure things behind one kind of "INT" or another?

But she wasn't done with Mr. Wallis yet as she continued, "And, you have told us previously that individual members of that organization in Southern Turkey have been known to subvert their own apparatus for personal reasons." She could see that he was about to interrupt but she just kept going, "And, you have told us that the rest of the group have been known to go along with anything that will embarrass Turkey, just because it would embarrass Turkey."

Bob looked like he was having a root canal done as Sheila continued, "So it is not unreasonable at all that someone, who might be a Kurd by birth, might accept a contract kill operation against one of our agents. All I did was share the observation that such a contract deal could have been brokered by someone they trust, like say the Kurd group inside Iran. You know the one who call themselves PJAK, which you have told us previously is, 'a politically active student group,' I believe was your previous assessment. It rather looks like they may be more than just politically active students. It looks like they may have become a full fledged player in the game!"

He tried to interject some comment but Sheila was still on a roll; and now she went for blood. "And speaking of intelligence, your guys did notice that Agent Johnson, you know Tango-3, has already been killed; and that Agent Kinderson, you know Tango-6, is also dead. And, now Tango-5, who has a vested interest in stopping this slaughter of operatives, has proposed a possible scenario. And you, without due consideration try to 'dismiss' his idea out of hand because it does not come from one of your 'INT' disciplines. In fact we haven't gotten jack-shit, pardon my language, from your high-tech world on this issue yet, have we?"

"Where were the warnings for Kinderson and for Johnson? Did you have anything productive to add? Or, are you more interested in poking holes in the only working theory on the table? I had hoped we might be able to expand or refine this raw piece of field work, or maybe come up with another theory." Then Sheila sat back and folded her arms across her chest.

Before Robert could respond, Tango Alpha raised his hands and said simply, "We are on a fifteen minute recess and then we will reconvene. Bring in any experts you need to. Then he stood and the room was in recess. Sheila went one way and Robert went the other.

Outside the room, Tango Alpha, "the old man," nodded to Sheila and said simply, "My office, please." But they both knew this was not a request.

The old man held the door for her to enter, wearing her business suit and house slippers. Once inside Sheila turned to face her Boss, "I am sorry, but he really is an ass and he hides behind his acronyms instead of expressing something constructive."

She quit talking abruptly when the old man held up one bent and gnarled index finger. He cleared his throat, "I was just going to say that I liked the way you took him apart in there." Then he smiled like a proud father or perhaps a trusted coach; but Sheila did not reply because he still held up the index finger. "But now that you have his attention, you need to direct his energies to give us something we can use, so no one else dies on the teams. Frankly, I am worried largely because we don't even have a clue who is doing this."

"Yes, sir." Sheila said as he crossed behind his desk and motioned her to sit in the chair across from the desk. She sat and then continued, "Bob wasn't out there when the bomb went off and Trav was. Trav shielded me from the blast and helped me recover from the initial shock and he is the one who got us both out of the kill zone."

"By the way," Tango Alpha cut in, "How are your feet?"

"Well they are a little cut up and bruised, and I am in serious need of a pedicure as soon as the last of the cuts heal." Then she added, "And the bastards who did this ruined a perfectly good pair of expensive shoes. Those were my favorite shoes too!"

Alpha laughed and Sheila smiled knowing he had enjoyed her joke. She was also just a little touched that he had asked. That meant he had already gotten the medical report from the scene on one of his people, her.

A few minutes later, they re-entered the room and saw that Wallis had brought re-enforcements. He had filled the chairs and brought some of his analysts along this time. Alpha took in the scene and said to Wallis, "Robert, the floor is yours."

"Thank you sir," And looking in Makinley's direction he uttered a one-word greeting, "Sheila." Then he cleared his throat and began, "In the interest of moving things along let's review the bidding on the things we know and see where the working theory might fit with or perhaps contradict the facts we know. As an ethnic group the Kurds originated in the Middle East and seem to like the Zagros Mountains. But the largest concentration is in that semi-autonomous region of Northern Iraq. That is the closest thing they have to a Kurdish state and there are about five million people living there. There are also concentrations in the neighboring regions of Syria, Iran and Turkey."

"Politically," he continued, "there does not appear to be a single unifying force except their insistence on an independent Kurdistan. There are multiple groups favoring, and sometimes supporting, varying degrees of political and/or military action. That brings us to the first point. The bomb that destroyed our vehicle was set so as to throw the vehicle away from the Hagia Sophia."

Bob Wallis looked to his team for assurances, and continued; "We think that is significant. To launch the vehicle as a burning wreck towards the museum could have been construed as a message of disrespect and disregard to the Islamic Leadership in Turkey. Hand in glove with that observation, is the fact that the random rifle fire did no significant damage, and did not hit any of our assets. The way the attack was conducted caused maximum embarrassment to the Turkish government and security forces. On the other hand it actually did minimum damage to any people or to the building itself."

"What we don't know is if the attack was aimed at a symbol of the establishment in general, i.e.: the car."

He took a breath, "Or, was the target Ms. Makinley and the operative she was contacting? If we assume the target was against specific people then the next question is who and why. The idea on the table, that it was a 'hit for hire,' is feasible."

"We say that," Wallis waved a hand indicating his staff, "since there are known and documented disconnects. And I might add, there are known and documented abuses by individual people within the various Kurdish factions. We know that because, there is certainly a cross flow of information. And we know there are black market operations between and among the Kurds in these geographically separate regions. So, in a word, 'yes,' a contract could have been issued through the Iranian Kurd community as a conduit to the group in Turkey asking for a targeted attack. It is, we conclude, a viable theory."

Sheila could see that it really pained Wallis to make this statement, which was really a concession, but she did not rub his face in it. What she did say was, "Bob, do we have any indications exactly who is assassinating our agents or why? Is there anything in the traffic that might help us get ahead of their next move?"

He looked almost sad as he sat down and said, "No, I am afraid not. I brought the senior analysts in for this session in hopes the discussion might trigger something with one of them." They all looked down at their hands folded on the table in a clear indication they had nothing to add. "But so far we have nothing. And yet whoever is doing this has demonstrated they are still ahead of us at every turn. It really implies a state actor or someone with the assets and approval of a state actor."

Sheila started to speak, but held herself in check as she heard the old man beside her clear his throat. "Of course it may mean all of these things and it may mean we have a leak inside our own processes." The room went quiet as that sank in. Then the old man continued, "It seems we have two tasks right now. The first is to find and stop the person or persons who are killing our operatives. The second task is to determine if there is a leak or an informant within the agency. Clearly you all understand that if there is no leak from inside the implied task is to find the source of the information and seal that leak. In other words how exactly are they able to get ahead of us?"

Back In The Field

Meanwhile, Harry Melon was driving across Turkey in an old Toyota Land Cruiser with a map, some basic supplies, a few weapons and a hunch. He was headed to Cizre, which is a city in Eastern Turkey located on the Tigris River. It is said to be the place where Alexander The Great crossed the Tigris. It was also a gateway for the Crusades when that religiously motivated military force was headed to Armenia from Mesopotamia around 639 AD.

Closer to more recent activities, in the nineteenth century Cizre was the site of a huge Kurdish rebellion against the Ottoman Empire. Kurds have been migrating to Cizre from diverse places for centuries and that migration continues today. Harry Melon's experience was that it is at such a cultural crossroads that one can find the greatest number of divergent political and economic influences intersecting.

It was an open secret, for example, that due in large part to its geography; this is where one can find support for the PKK and for the YPG, as well as other interests officially outlawed in modern-day Turkey.

Thousands of Yezidi refugees, and Syrian refugees of Kurdish stock, have come to the region and found a home of sorts. Those families are still there and still biding their time and waiting for the opportunities that might lead to the creation of their own homeland.

It is said that a westerner cannot understand the Kurds unless one is a Kurd and the only place to understand the Kurds is to be in Kurdistan. That dream of a homeland does not yet exist but the hope is alive in Cizre. This is what Harry Melon was hoping for as he drove along on a road to nowhere. But he hoped the journey would lead him to find the one thread, the one loose end, that might unravel this whole "thing." This "thing" after all threatened his existence and had wrecked havoc on his agency.

His gut told him that Russians were involved in some way; and made him think about the cultural attaché's office in Frankfurt. As he drove along he remembered Sonja and her helpers who had almost taken him out a few years ago. But, logic told him, that was about five years ago, and five years was an eternity in this business.

Besides, since then the attaché had been replaced by the old guy's assistant, Alfred or Albert or something like that. He would have to check that first chance he got. Besides, since then, or more accurately since that incident, the Cultural Attaché's Office had gone quiet and seemed to be a non-problem these days. And, now that he was thinking about it, Sergei had died in an auto accident back in Russia, as he recalled. But right now he needed to focus on driving to Cizre and what he was going to do when he got there.

Chapter 5: Cizre

The Jazirat Ibn 'Umar was a town located in the nether regions, north of Mosul, in the time when Christian Crusades came through the region. But that was only a passing thing; it was but a moment in history. Before, and after, this time the political and financial power brokers in he region were known to have maintained personal as well as trade ties and business arrangements with many very diverse groups. In fact from the 12th century, cartographers of that era have left amazingly accurate maps, with notations showing more than four thousand Jews residing in the area. The area called Cizre was a melting pot of peoples and a mixing bowl of cultures, ideas and interests a long, long time ago. That condition continues today.

Many Americans believe that the melting pot concept originated with the creation of the United States, but the truth is it predates the New World by centuries. The lesson for us today is that those influences have deep roots if we are to understand today's politics. In other words, forces and interests that may not be readily visible today have influenced, and continue to influence today's political realities. It is sometimes prudent, some would say necessary, to dive deeply into those almost forgotten histories. And a look at those maps is always instructive.

For example the Jazirat Ibn 'Umar was built by al-Hasan Ibn Umar, who was the Emir of Mosul at the time. He is given the credit for conceiving of, and constructing the city in the 9th century. This is all the more remarkable because it was built on a man-made island, in the middle of the Tigris River. Most of the true believers would argue that, located as it is near the Ararat Mountains, puts everyone living there now near to where Noah's Ark came to rest. The locals also "know" that Umar Ibn al-Khattab, the person, had made a mosque out of Noah's Ark, using its wood to frame the mosque.

Oblivious to all of this at the moment and moving as someone with a purpose, Travis was maneuvering through the outskirts of Cizre. The neighborhood he was walking through is in the Kurdish region of modern day Turkey. The Kurds call the city Cizir and it is located as previously noted on the Tigris River near the border with Syria and Iraq. And, as we have also noted it is reputed to be the final resting place of Noah. Travis walked along looking for a location he had not visited in a decade. He was searching for his old academic professor and mentor, Aferin, whose name ironically meant "trustworthy."

Doctor, Professor, Aferin Abbas had made his home in Cizre as his professional career had wound down at the university in Germany where Travis had studied under him. He had joked at the time with his students, one of whom was a younger Charles Travis Lemon, that his last name Abbas meant "austere" and that it was more a curse than it was a blessing. "After all," he would say, "I have spent my productive life in academia where one does not grow rich. And now as I prepare for retirement I am headed for a homeland that does not yet exist except in our hearts."

But Travis knew there were also other powerful forces driving the aging professor. Included in these forces was that Cizre was widely believed to be where

Alexander The Great had crossed the Tigris. And, the old city had been a gateway for The Crusaders to access Armenia from Mesopotamia. As if that were not enough, in 639 AD it had been chosen as the seat of the Syriac Orthodox Church. And more to the point for Travis today it had been the site of a huge Kurdish rebellion against the Ottoman Empire in the 19th century. The draw and the attraction of all this for a serious academic researcher, like Aferin Abbas, was obvious; and the draw for Travis was the presence of Aferin Abbas.

Politically, that historical resistance continued today against the successor political state called The Republic of Turkey. The remaining population in this region continues to be almost all Kurdish, and it is close to similar populations in Iraq and Syria in terms of distance. And of course, ideologically it is close to the university-trained elites in Iran who are proud to declare that they are Kurdish.

Travis knew that about one in ten of these families had loved ones who were fighting with the Kurdistan Workers Party, PKK. In the near future those same families would send their youth to fight with the Kurdish YPG fighting against a new threat that was yet to come. That threat would emerge from a group that would call itself ISIS in the not too distant future. But that was to be in the future, and right now those forces were still being formulated as a concept and recruited to shape a new reality.

His personal focus right now, at this point in time, was searching for the retirement home of Professor Aferin Abbas, his "trustworthy and austere" old mentor. Travis was meandering through the old part of the city, which had obviously been bombarded more than once by modern weapons, as he finally found the old building. Mercifully this neighborhood had escaped the worst of the sporadic violence and looked to be largely intact, relatively speaking.

The people he noted even displayed some items of western dress. So, mixed in among local women in full hijab, he could see some ladies who wore a colorful scarf, but only around their hair; and always, always in long modest dresses. Men on the other hand wore a mix of western slacks and shirts mixed with the more traditional garb. Meanwhile the youth, young men and sometimes women, could be seen in groups wearing elements of camouflage clothing. For the young men this meant uniform shirts and pants. And for the young women this meant a uniform shirt, almost as someone in the West might wear a sweater or a jacket. He had also observed the two fit young men who were trailing him although one appeared to have temporarily disappeared.

"Ah," Travis thought, "there he is." This came just as that one stepped into his path, and the other one came up behind him.

"What is it you want?" The man facing him demanded with a note of arrogance in his voice. Trav noticed that he was also pretending to conceal a weapon in his belt under his shirt. It was so badly hidden that Trav could only surmise the young man wanted everyone to see; so they would know he was dangerous. He was obviously an idiot.

Travis was more interested in the man behind him who had not appeared to be carrying a weapon. That could mean he was unarmed, but more likely it meant he was in charge, and he actually knew how to conceal a weapon. Of the two, the second man would be the one who was really dangerous.

Travis turned his back on the first young man in an obvious insult and answered the question to the second man behind him. "I seek Professor Aferin, and I come in peace."

The man he was facing opened his mouth to speak but, as Travis suspected would happen, the other man made his move. He placed a hand on Trav's shoulder from behind and commanded, "Do not turn your back on me, infidel!"

Travis pivoted to the left turning into the thug's arm and inside his space almost face to face. He simultaneously brought the first two fingers of his right hand up in a "V" formation and jammed a finger into each of the man's nostrils. Besides the immediate shock effect, the force of the thrust, brought the man's head up and back in an involuntary reflex action as he tried to get away from the pain in his nose.

Travis balled his left hand into a fist and drove a hammer blow into the man's groin. That blow doubled him over forward and as he fell past, Travis grabbed the pistol from the man's belt under his shirt. The man behind Travis started to react but stopped when he saw Travis hold the pistol in the air with his right and eject the clip, as he jacked the slide to eject the round that was in the chamber. Then he turned the pistol around butt first and handed it to the fellow behind him and said, "I seek Professor Aferin, and I come in peace."

From over their heads the two heard the sound of a man clapping his hands slowly together. And as they looked up across the street to the balcony, Travis saw his old mentor clapping as if to give an ovation. He also noticed the two gunmen on either side of Aferin who held their weapons at the ready but not aiming at anyone. "Travis! Is that you? It has been so long. Please come up and chat," his old professor shouted and turned to go back into the building.

"Shall we go up?" The man behind Travis asked.

"What about your friend?" Travis asked indicating the other young man who was starting to recover.

Trav's escort said with an edge to his voice, "He is not my friend. I thought he was with you." Then, smiling at his little joke he added, "Besides he needs more training and a little humility." Travis only nodded and the man said, "Can I ask you a personal question?"

Travis replied, "Yes, but I may decide not to answer it."

"That is fair enough." The man said and then continued, "I saw your eyes when he called you an infidel..."

"But," Travis cut him off, "I am not an infidel." Travis let that sink in and added, "I assume you follow the prophet Mohammed, peace of Allah be upon him, is that correct?" The man nodded and Travis continued as he had been taught so many years before, "I follow a different Prophet. His name is Jesus. So we both are 'children of the book' and just following different prophets. Thus neither of us is a 'non-believer' nor an infidel."

"Thank you." The man said, "That is a logical answer." They entered the doorway in silence and the man gestured up stairs although he waited back outside the door to the stairs.

Looking up to the first landing Travis saw his old mentor holding out his arms in a greeting and smiling. As Travis climbed the stairs the man said, "As I live and breath Charles Travis Lemon! What are you doing and why have you gone to all this trouble come and see me? Please come inside and we can talk a while." Then turning to his two bodyguards he said simply, "Leave us a while please."

The guard did not like that, based on the expression on his face, and he said, "We must search him for a weapon."

Aferin turned on the guard and said a little louder, "Did you not see what he did on the street downstairs? If he has a weapon or not, he does not need one to harm an old man like me. So please humor me and let me talk privately with my former student." The guards frowned but they turned and left the room empty except for Travis and Aferin.

The older man shrugged to Travis and asked, "Can I offer you some tea? I was just about to make some for myself."

"That would be lovely, sir." Then Travis added, "In fact it would be almost like the days back at the university. Drinking tea and coming to consult with you for answers to my problems forms one of my fondest memories."

"But your problems then were academic, my young friend." Aferin said over his shoulder from the sink. "I suspect your problems now are more related to the real world."

"They are," Trav agreed, and added, "But let's have our first cup of tea and remember other times. Maybe by cup two or three we can get around to my modest problems."

"You see!" The old man smiled, "You never forget anything. It does take three cups of tea to become a friend; but we are already friends, so as you say, maybe on the next cup." Then walking back with the tea in cups the old man added, "How are you doing? Do you have a wife or a woman? And, do you have children?" Travis noted the old man did not ask why he was there and he honestly did not know if that is because he already knew, or because he was sticking to the old custom common in so much of the region.

After an hour or so of conversation, Travis noted that the old man smiled almost sadly whenever he mentioned Julie. But he made no reaction when Trav said he did not yet have any children. Eventually the conversation made its way around to the reason for Trav's visit.

"Professor, someone tried to kill me the other day in Istanbul with a bomb attached to a car." Trav noted there was no surprise in the old man's face as he continued adding, " I was walking in the company of a woman," Travis saw the old man raise an eyebrow and he quickly added, "She is a work colleague and we were walking from my favorite building in that city, the Hagia Sophia. We were headed to a car her driver had parked a respectful distance from the old building. But our meeting was cut short because the car suddenly exploded and was thrown into the air by the force of the blast."

Aferin started to speak but Trav held up a finger asking to be allowed to continue, "The bomb was obviously larger than it had to be. Of course that means to me that someone wanted to send a signal. The goal was not just to destroy a car, nor to kill either of us. And the bomb was placed in a perfect spot to launch the car away from the Hagia Sophia and not towards the building. That was likely on purpose as well, so as not to show a signal of disrespect for the Muslim leadership in Istanbul. And at the same time the whole thing would become a huge embarrassment to the Turkish Government, even if it failed to kill any person."

The old man sucked in an audible breath but allowed Travis to continue. "In my mind there is a short list of people or groups who have the capability and the desire to cause such embarrassment. At the top of the list are certain elements of the Kurdish movement."

The old man spoke this time. "And in your mind, how and why could this have happened as you suggest?"

Travis spoke slowly and carefully, "I suspect someone, from Iran, may have found a way to coerce, or co-opt and mislead, the Kurdish student movement at the university in Iran. Perhaps that group was then used to transmit a false message to the Kurdish organizations that clearly might have the training, equipment and willingness to embarrass the Turks. If I am right then the Iranians wanted a death and were disappointed. But the Kurds would have been satisfied with taking their money, and their weapons, while causing an embarrassment to the Turks. In fact supporting their purposes it would further demonstrate and highlight Turkish inability to control and govern as a legitimate organization."

Travis picked up his teacup and sat back in the chair.

"You have not asked for anything." Aferin said softly.

"You, professor, will tell me what you want to tell me and what you can tell me. You always have, and we both know there are no simple answers in this world. I can only offer you the respect of waiting while you decide what you can, or what you will say."

This time the professor picked up his teacup and sat back looking at his former student and assessing the man he had become. "As you say. Sip your tea and give me a moment to organize my words. Then I will make another cup of tea for us both and we will talk."

Chapter 6: View From Madrid vs View From Cizre

The Intelligence Steering Group Meeting for Tango Section, at the Embassy Compound in Madrid, had concluded leaving a sour taste in everyone's mouth. Wallis and his team had left first because Tango Alpha had dismissed them. As they left he told Sheila to remain behind for a short high level discussion. She sat obediently as he requested, with her face impassive, as the intelligence experts exited the secure room.

When the door closed again, the old man turned to her and said quietly, "We will wait here a few minutes then I would like you to join me in my office for a real discussion."

Sheila's face held an unspoken question but all she said was, "As you wish."

Then the old man slid a piece of paper over to her, on which was written, 'I will explain later. Just scribble something on this page and pass it back to me.'

Sheila picked up on the game immediately and wrote 'OK why are we not talking?'

Tango Alpha quickly scribbled, 'Projection booth.'

"Yes, sir!" Sheila said with a good semblance of enthusiasm in her voice, "I agree." Then she made a show of signing the paper with a flourish and put the cap on her pen and placed it back in the little holder on her notepad. Finally she folded the paper and almost ceremoniously handed it back to her Director.

Tango Alpha refolded the paper and placed it into his inside jacket pocket. "All right, then." He said standing and inclining his head toward the door, "Come with me please." His voice was flat and without emotion but what he was thinking was that he wanted to laugh out loud. This little charade should give Wallis and his spies something to spend the rest of the day conjecturing and worrying about. He led the way down a hallway and past his outer office receptionist, who looked up but did not speak, and through the heavy doors into his private office with Sheila Makinley in tow.

When they were inside the office and the door was closed, Sheila said simply, "Sir?"

"Sit down and relax a moment." Tango Alpha said. "That little show served my purposes; because, it is occasionally good to remind the staff, especially the intelligence bureaucrats, who they support and why they are here."

He paused and Sheila said, "So, that is why you held me behind 'for Steering Committee' business?"

"Exactly and that little bit at the end where you signed your name was a nice piece of theater. That will have them wondering all day as to exactly what you just agreed to." She started to speak but he held up a finger to stop her, "From the bureaucrat's perspective there is always the fear that one's enemies will be put in charge of your empire. That looked a lot like you had just signed off on accepting responsibility for something important. Robert is not and never was a field agent. He has come entirely out of the intelligence world of high tech and the exquisite toys they employ."

He took a breath but she could tell this was not the time to interrupt, "Sheila, do not misunderstand, Bob is smart. No, more accurately, Bob is brilliant. But he has just never developed the 'field instincts' that people like you and Travis and Naja have. I do not pretend to know if you developed it over time or if you were born with it but it is essential in this business and especially at a time like this. Specifically, it is critical when it appears to be open season on our field operatives. Robert does not have a 'gut' to trust. Do you remember the shift in his attitude during the previous session?"

This she knew required an answer. "Yes. As soon as he came back into the room with his section heads for support he became almost conciliatory, didn't he? I wondered about that."

"Yes," the old man said, "That is when I remembered the old projection booth behind that little window behind us. Have you ever been in that booth?"

"I have seen it and I know it is there but not often in use." Sheila started but he cut her off.

"It is not in use often for briefings anymore but, trust me, three people can squeeze into it and two of them can put their heads together and see into the room. And all can hear every word said." The old man sat back and let that sink in.

Sheila just sat there a moment and smiled. Then she said quietly, "And how much do I owe you in tuition for this little class?"

He smiled as well, "The fact that you realize its value is all the compensation I require."

"But you put the pieces together from Robert's change of attitude." Sheila shook her head in wonder at the bureaucratic force the old man must have been, and likely still was. She would not want to face off against him in a budget fight or a policy debate back in DC.

"By the way," he added, "Travis is the one who pointed it out to me a long, long time ago."

At that Sheila let a little laugh escape her lips then became very serious and said simply, "I pray he is OK and I hope he has success with what he has going on out in the field right now."

"As a mater of policy we give the '"Tango-series'" operatives a lot of latitude in operations and focus on their results. But frankly, Sheila, we have very little else to hang our hat on right now. The 'Roberts of the world' are trying everything they can think of, but frankly there may be nothing further to intercept. This is looking very 'old school' where everything goes from mouth-to-ear and hand-to-hand. And electronics cannot help with that." Tango Alpha only paused a second then said, "We have already lost two operatives and of course there was the attempt on you and Travis. This has effectively paralyzed the field operations as the people out there keep an eye looking behind themselves and their loved ones."

They both sat in silence a moment longer then Sheila rose and said., "If that is all, sir."

"Yes," he smiled, "Go back to work and see if you can come up with anything that might help Travis, and the others out in the field. I would welcome anything that might help us neutralize this threat."

Meanwhile In Cizre

School was no longer in session; Ex-professor Aferin Abbas, PhD had effectively told Travis what he knew and what he conjectured. For Travis it was almost like being back at the university. The Professor was frustratingly famous among the students for not actually answering a question. Rather he would always provide information and lead the student to draw his or her own conclusions on matters, and then make their own decisions, especially on the difficult matters.

"Travis, there is much you know and much you understand but there is also much more that you do not yet know and do not yet understand. Additionally there is much you will never know and therefore can never understand. There are maybe five hundred thousand or six hundred thousand Kurds in Germany. These people are scattered in cities like Hamburg, Munich, Frankfurt, Stuttgart and Essen as guest workers."

"Or, if you prefer they are called 'gastarbeiters' by the Germans. There is a huge flow of people in and out of Germany, quite legally, every day. And over time, more and more of them stay in Germany because there is work to do and money to be made. And, I need not add that there is therefore, money to be sent back to Kurds in places like this." The professor took another sip of his tea and then continued. "To a lesser extent there is similar activity in Italy too but the numbers are smaller by a factor of ten; so maybe twenty five thousand."

"But, my young friend, relevant to your problem right now, those hundreds of thousands of Kurdish people are first and foremost 'people.' They are individuals and they are motivated by causes and by values that are important to them. And, that is a very personal thing, and it is equally hard to discern. Admittedly, by human nature, they seek out others who have similar interests, and similar values, or those who may be able to take advantage of similar situations." Aferin noted a growing restlessness on the face of his friend and former student as he took a sip of his tea before going on.

"Travis, do not be blinded by impatience." Aferin admonished the younger man. "There are also, in

Germany over two hundred thousand Iranians. These are also gastarbeiters and they are working in Germany for the same reasons. They are doing some of the same jobs and therefore most likely are in contact with each other." Aferin could see this information had an impact on Travis as the younger man sat back in his chair and sipped his own tea a little more patiently as his mind churned.

"These Iranians also are motivated by different individual interests and concerns that are personal to them individually. Some of them are also Kurdish." He paused half a minute for impact and repeated himself. "Some of them are also Kurds. This is where you are going to find significant numbers of disaffected, and maybe even a little bit lonely. They will be seeking individuals and groups; and these groups will be reaching out to them, offering contact with others who have similar values and goals and dreams."

"This large movement of people into and out of Germany has taken a significant jump since about 1980. But these two groups go to places where they can find countrymen and receive help and assistance from people they feel that they can trust. The one city where Turkish gastabeiters, including Kurds, and where Iranians, again including Kurds, gather in relatively close contact, is currently in Frankfurt."

"Frankfurt!" Travis said sounding a bit incredulous. "Really?"

"That is where they can find work for which they have the skills. That is where they can find friendly reception from countrymen already there living among a German population who only see them as 'gastarbeiters.' The Germans are seeing them yet not seeing them. And no one is making a distinction between Iranian, and Turk, or Kurd, and non-Kurd. So, that is where they are invisible, and as the Americans say, they are below the radar, and they are hiding in plain sight. If the estimates are to be believed there may be three hundred and fifty to four hundred thousand Turks in Frankfurt and the surrounding area. And these are all thrown together in the same place but they are very different people."

"There is rail, and there are roads, and there is an international airport. It is also very industrialized and there are political entities there representing 'big-power' nation states." Then Aferin put his teacup down and said simply. "I have given you what I know and now I give you my speculation that your theory is plausible. You should take your search to that city and start looking in earnest. The answer lies between Frankfurt and Dresden."

"Dresden?" Travis said, surprised again.

Aferin repeated and continued, "The answer lies between Frankfurt and Dresden. The people have no home and dreams of home are a powerful motivator. They are divided by political boundaries and geography. They have found a homeland in their minds but it is not yet a reality on the Earth. Such people can be misled by their dreams and desires and by those who are untrustworthy. There are untrustworthy people working and living in Dresden for their government and for the KGB."

"KGB?" Travis said aloud.

"There have been recent transfers of former KGB people into Dresden from Moscow and these people are unscrupulous. They have already caused problems for Kurds and Turks in both Germanys. It is a dangerous mixture." Aferin said, and added, "The innocence of dreams and hopes, the money and resources from Frankfurt, and the direction of plots and manipulations from Dresden. It is a dangerous mixture."

"While you Americans were being 'busy' in other parts of the world, the Brits and the Russians came together in Iran but never left during the last power transition. When the dust settled, the people, the Kurds, still do not have a home. When the Shah came to power, the Brits went back to watching from afar. But, my friend, the Russians never left and they are still engaged."

"Travis, I say again, go and look in Germany. The GDR may be too hard to enter and leave but the FRG is easily within your reach. And the people who may have provided motivation for that horrendous act that threatened your life, will not be satisfied with a lack of success. They will try again my friend. If they failed with efforts to subvert the Kurdish movement for their own ends then they will try another angle. But, as you already know, you are fighting a shadow adversary who has funding and resources on a regional, and maybe a global scale. They are not done, my young friend; and frankly I enjoy your visits even if they do not come so often anymore."

Travis said his goodbyes and left knowing that Aferin had answered most if not all of his questions. Interestingly he had done it in a way that gave Travis quantifiable data that he could feed to the intelligence machine back at HQ. All of these things could be quantified and verified by Bob Wallis and his experts.

Funny, mused Travis, how Bob and his experts could verify almost anything but even with all the pieces in front of them they did not often see the whole picture. On the other hand, one old man sipping tea and thinking had put pieces together. And yet, Aferin himself, had not broken any vows of silence to any group and could not be quoted as a source for any of the information derived from the data. Travis wondered for just a passing second if his former professor had ever worked for a governmental agency.

But Travis did not have long to consider as he came out of the building and the same two men were waiting for him at the bottom of the stairs. The one had a bandage on his nose and his weapon was much more discretely positioned under is shirt. He stepped forward and for a split second Travis thought he was up for another lesson in street fighting. But the man stepped forward, placed his right hand over his heart and said only "Peace be with you."

Travis returned the same gesture and replied, "And with you, and may God smile upon you and all your loved ones."

The fellow actually smiled and extended his hand in the western fashion. Travis took his hand in a firm but friendly grip and then turned to the other man, "Thank you both for helping me have a delightful afternoon with my old friend and teacher. Please take care of him because the work you all do is important."

At that the other man offered his hand and they all parted company in a non-hostile way. Travis kept his awareness at a high pitch. He knew he would have time to reflect in detail on the long drive back across Turkey until he could catch a plane to Germany. He would also have time to stop at the Air Base in Incirlik where he could find secure communication and a safe place to rest for a night.

Chapter 7: Reflecting On All He Heard

He lay awake in a modestly furnished room for visitors in the Bachelor Officer's Quarters on Incirlik Air Base. Travis found himself lying here, in a bed that was too small and too hard, at a US Air Base in Turkey, staring at the ceiling and still sorting out the details. He had replayed every nuance of the conversation and discussion with his old mentor, Aferin Abbas.

In many ways it made sense and Tavis could see the connections begin to form. Of course he also realized that at this point they were spotty and sometimes tenuous. And yet, they also made sense after a fashion and should be explored. That was his job; he was the one best positioned to explore them.

He also was not sure that having someone else look for the connections would do any good at all. After all, he knew what he was looking for, and there was still the chance he would miss a critical piece or a key connection. Passing this to someone else for follow up would just make the whole process less efficient.

The Federal Republic of Germany, the FRG, more commonly just referred to as "West Germany" had become one of the major manufacturing engines that drove the economy of continental Western Europe after World War II. Not surprisingly there were US as well as Russian and Soviet interests competing in every way that they could compete in the region on a daily basis. Then there were the "guest workers" whose numbers had surged and were still surging throughout the region.

This influx of ethnic groups of workers all sponsored each other, and their family and friends, getting set up. They helped each other with work opportunities and housing; and provided a plethora ot of mini-ethnic environments of all flavors. When these people arrived they found a place to be comfortable in their adopted home and even a status of sorts in the German society as a "guest worker."

And more to the point there were at least two hundred thousand ex-Pat Iranians in Germany which meant a significant number of Kurds as well. And the Kurds are after all one of the largest minority groups in Iran. In fact they, and the Iranian-Azerbaijanis, together also made up over a tenth of the total Iranian population.

And yet Ravis knew, the Kurds themselves may have had more in common politically with the Armenians as the tensions grew and escalated in the Nagorno-Karabakh region of Azerbaijan. In point of fact the Armenian population dominated that particular area of the world as the majority population under a minority rule. Of course, at least on a regional basis, that meant unusual affiliations and friendships and relationships could be expected to flourish, and they did. The Kurds just wanted action and movement towards a homeland despite the different approaches of the PKK, the KDP, the PJAK and the plethora of other groups. They all shared a desire for an independent Kurdistan. And that meant they were susceptible to being manipulated.

Russian Influence

Travis came to the realization that Aferin must have been correct. The hub of all this had to be in Frankfurt! All the elements came together there; but

Aferin had also made a good point about the Russians. Russian influence was greatest in the GDR; and the GDR, ironically was also a major pain the butt for Moscow politics. The two political leaderships did not share the same vision.

Of course Russian political succession had always been a matter of art not science! The economic reforms of Yuri Andropov enacted in 1973 and in 1979 had brought mixed results. And the short-lived Troika, Led by Konstantin Chernenko, who replaced him, fell apart with just a year in office. This was in part due to the poor health of the members, and the death of Dimitry Ustinov.

In the end the Troika served only about a year from February 1984 to March 1985. Then on 10 March 1985 Moscow entered a period of relative stability amid change as Mikhail Gorbachev took office and implemented his programs for Perestroika. Amidst this fluid situation and Honecker's longevity, some in Moscow felt it prudent to put people in the GDR who might be able to get Honecker, and everyone else, back in line with Russian interests.

The challenge was to send in someone who was capable and motivated but not on the international radar; and it needed to not be located in the Capitol of East Berlin. That person was Vladimir Putin and he was dispatched to Dresden with authorities, responsibilities and links to Moscow that he needed. And, as the planners intended, it was far enough removed from Berlin that if there were a misstep and the whole thing blew up in their faces, it was easier to cover it all up. Any problems could be made to look like an overly aggressive operative gone rogue in the political backwater of Dresden. It could even be made to look like an East-West Germany plot of some sort to further muddy the water.

One thing was for sure; whatever Putin did in Dresden on this new mission, it was not a political backwater to East Germany. Therefore it was going to be a key to future engagement for NATO in the Central European theater of operations. And that was all Putin needed to know as he extended his authorities to the mission in West Germany. After all these were really just cover for intelligence operations, as Alfred was finding out almost daily.

The Phone Call

And as usually seems to happen, just as Travis was finally unwinding physically as well as form his mental sorting process an urgent sounding knock startled him awake. "Sir. Mr. Travis. Sir, it's important." The voice on the other side of the door said.

Travis opened the door, feeling relatively safe in the BOQ on this little piece of American sovereignty. He saw a young Sergeant standing outside his door looking a little worried and maybe a little confused. "Yes." Travis said, "Can I help you, Sergeant?"

"Sir, The OD, I mean Officer of the Day on duty, in the Command Post sent me to get you." The young man said somewhat cryptically.

"And, may I ask why?" Travis said keeping his voice flat but clearly interested in the answer.

"Oh, yes sir. Sorry, sir. I should have started with that. There was a call over a secure line in the CP from somebody important. They said they needed to talk with you as soon as possible. Can you come with me, please?" The flustered young man said with an underlying tone of urgency.

The Command Post

Ten minutes later Travis was being escorted into the Air Base Operations Center much like every other Operations Center in which he had worked over the years. There were the ever-present Plexiglas boards, backlit to show the aircraft and systems status and on-call contact names and numbers in the event of a need to call someone. After the appropriate security and ID checks, Major White, who seemed to be in charge, offered Travis a seat at his console. "Mr. Travis, there is a secure call that you are supposed to return to a lady named Sheila who said she has some information for your ears only."

They were in a sort of raised room with its own array of communications consoles and electronics but the walls were all clear glass. From here the Officer of the Day could oversee the entire operations room as well as maintain situation awareness of the information flow. It looked like there might be four or five people occupying this space on a day shift but just the one officer on the night shift.

Maj. White now had Trav's attention. "I understand, Major White, is there a phone system I can use?"

"Yes, sir. This room is pretty much soundproof despite the glass walls and I will step out if you need privacy." The Major responded.

"Isn't that a little unusual?" Travis asked out of curiosity.

"Yes, sir, it is. But the line on which the lady called and the precedence with which the call came in is way above my pay grade. So, whatever it is you are into, it must be some really heavy shit." Then catching himself, the Maj. he self-corrected, "I meant to say it must be some really high level stuff."

"No, I think you had it right the first time. And, by the way, I am a former Air Force Officer myself. So I feel like I am among friends; but yes, I will ask you to step out because you do not want any part of what I am doing. Trust me on that one." Travis answered but with a smile on his face.

"OK then, let me get you connected and I will go refresh my coffee cup. Then I need to make my routine checks on the guys on the floor below us." With that Major White made the connections, passed the phone handset to Travis and exited the OD's room.

When the room was clear, "Sheila? This is Trav. This is an unexpected surprise."

"Hi Trav. I came across something that might be of use." Came Sheila's voice on the other end of the communications line sounding a little garbled on some words as the encryption occasionally did not synch properly.

"Good! I will take all the input I can get!" Trav answered.

"Well," Sheila began, "do you remember that fellow you killed in El Salvador so many years ago?" But she clearly did not expect a reply nor did she wait for one, "Well his name was Nikolai Ivanovich and his father was Sergei Ivanovich. Ivanovich was assigned as the Cultural Attaché working out of Russia's Frankfurt, Germany Office."

Trav felt those icy fingers on the back of his neck again as his gut instincts sensed alarm, "You have my attention. We have dealt with Sergei before not long ago. But I heard he retired and then died in an auto crash."

"Exactly. Yes, he has in fact retired and, he did die in a car accident when his brakes failed." Sheila took a breath and then pressed on, "Anyhow, his former assistant is a weasel of a man named Alfred, and Alfred replaced Sergei in the office."

"OK, so far interesting information but not a clear linkage." Travis said.

"Always so impatient, I am just coming to that." Sheila replied, "We came by this data quite by accident."

"That's always how the best stuff comes to the surface," Travis interjected, "by accident."

"Well, that is true, but be that as it may," Sheila continued, "we got a cross flow notification from another agency that monitors police investigations and it seems that Alfred has made it onto someone's radar. He has a pretty young agent named Svetlana working for him. It appears she has a taste for items on the rationed list in Germany, you know, cigarettes, coffee, gas, and stuff like that."

Travis knew it well from his days living as a young Officer living on the economy and using a ration card every week, "Yep, not uncommon." He said.

"Well in a side note it seems that Alfred may have put her up to it as some kind of test to see if she could put together a little ration card smuggling business. Of course for her this would be minor but if an established and credentialed diplomat, like Alfred, is behind it calling the shots then we can use that later to exert pressure or to influence him."

Travis was becoming a little impatient and said so, "Sheila, can you get to the point please?"

"OK here goes. Our friends, who watch Russians in Germany, have told us that Alfred also has inherited Sergei's old contact list which includes the family of an Iranian member of the IRGC." Sheila paused for effect.

"Now you have my full attention! I am listening." Travis said with obvious enthusiasm in his voice.

"And it seems the Iranian, a guy named Farouq, was a classmate with Nikolai at the technical school that Russia runs to prep their field operatives. And this fellow, Farouq, has family in Germany, and first Sergei, and now Alfred keep an eye on the family. He even visits them routinely, so there is ongoing contact. It may be a stretch but, since I don't believe in 'coincidences,' I thought this might tie in with our problem at the moment?"

Travis then, when it was his turn to talk, gave her great detail on his discussions with his old mentor and outlined roughly what he was thinking and pursuing. Sheila shared with him that there were other ideas being considered, but they had nothing that sounded any more credible than what he was on. Almost as an afterthought, Travis said "Oh, and if you can, have Bob pry into any new Russian Ops in Dresden. That was the last thing my old mentor said to me, that 'The road to Moscow goes through Dresden,' and the old guy is seldom wrong."

Sheila said she would and then she wrapped up with, "Trav, the whole agency is walking on egg shells wondering who will be next in line to be killed. I will get word to you of anything else we stumble across here. Good luck out there."

"Sheila," Travis said finally, "I sincerely appreciate what you have put together. This is indeed a big help, almost like the old days again except the stakes are a lot higher this time."

Sheila agreed and Travis disconnected just as Major White came back in with a fresh cup of coffee in his mug and a second cup he offered to Travis. "Get you business all done?" he asked Tavis.

"Yep. And I appreciate the hospitality. But I will be gone quickly and should not be bothering you and your people again any time soon. And thanks for the coffee too."

"No problem. You know where we are if you need more support. Can I ask who you actually work for?" The Maj. Asked.

"You can ask but I would have to lie to you because the people I work for are not 'on the books' as the saying goes." Travis replied honestly. Then thoughtfully, Travis added, "Why? You looking for a job, Major White?"

"No, sir. I am very close to retirement, that is of course if I count credit for my enlisted time." Then he added, "Maybe it would be nice to have something to keep me busy in my retired years." The Officer of the Day said simply.

"Well, then maybe I will pass your name along to some friends. We may have a few openings to fill in the near future." And with that Travis let the topic drop.

"That's about what I thought. I think I ran into a few of your people back when I was spending time in and out of Nam." And with that the two men shook hands and parted company. The young Sergeant appeared from nowhere and escorted Travis back to his BOQ room.

A few hours later Travis woke feeling almost rested and with some fresh ideas to pursue. He would head back to Germany and find his old contact in the Border Police.

Chapter 8: West German Border Police

The political realities at the end of World War II brought many changes to the diplomatic landscape of the world, especially in Europe. Among these changes was the desire, among many nations, that certain "aggressor-nations" focus their attentions inward and not look outward, ever again! In the end, after all the political machinations, the world had a Japan which does not have a military per se. They do have a Japanese Defense Force whose stated purpose is defense and protection, as opposed to aggressive external military action.

In the same vein, and for the same reasons, another of these "constrained-nations" is Germany. The Post-War Germany's goals, in the international arena, are now aimed at protection of their homeland, and the reunification of the greater German State. And frankly no one wanted to see another mechanism for internal national control like that of the various appendages of the NAZI political, paramilitary and military movement.

The system that emerged is a very traditional police force along with very traditional law enforcement agencies in the FRG. Consequently West Germany was unfortunately, singularly unprepared to respond effectively to the Palestinian terrorist attack a few years later. A Palestinian terror group who called themselves "Black September" became infamous with one horrific act.

On the 5th of September in 1972 during the Munich, West Germany, Olympic Games this Palestinian group attacked and kidnapped, or in some cases, killed athletes. These athletes were in the FRG for the sole purpose of competing in the Games. Black September killed two of these young people inside the Olympic Village. They also kidnapped 11 Israeli athletes before the German Police could even mount an effective response. However, the German Police were neither trained now equipped for this type of internal domestic para-military operation.

In the end the whole operation was a disaster that resulted in many unnecessary deaths of innocents, and a major political embarrassment for the FRG leadership. The Police had badly underestimated the number of terrorists. And, among other errors, the Police did not even have a sniper team who could have effectively engaged the terrorists. Of course the German military did have these capabilities, but the Post-War German Constitution did not allow such action by the military on German soil in peacetime.

The "fix action" to rectify this debacle was to pass the task to a unit of the German Border police. These Border Patrol units were often referred to as the "Gruenzschutz" or "green legs" because of the distinctive green strip on the legs of their leather pants. The task fell to the Border Police Group number 9, which became known as Gruenzschutzgruppe (GSG9) of the Bundespolizei. This political artifice worked well since the Border Police functioned in a fashion similar to a Gendarmerie that straddles both Police and Military capabilities in the execution of their assigned duties.

The GSG9 was a successful concept put into action and quickly became the "go to" agency in cases involving hostage taking, and kidnapping. It also quickly took on counter-terrorism, extortion and high-risk cases involving organized crime. As it continues to evolve it has taken on the still emerging cyber-crime challenges of the modern world. The checks and balances in place have meant that GSG9 only functions in conditions where the local elected authorities have sanctioned such activity. In this way all the political boxes have been checked.

As important as all this background is, perhaps of more direct interest to our story here are the little known connections with the US military from the infancy of GSG9. They did some of their training and research in Fulda, Germany at the Downs Barracks, Fulda Army Kasserne, Fulda Germany. Literally on the next mountain over was a USAF Radar Station on the Wasserkuppe. Many of the officers and families who lived in the town of Fulda used those same facilities routinely. It would not be a stretch of the imagination to think that a young Air Force Officer named Charles Travis Lemon met, and played ball, and drank beer with a young Police Officer named

Hans Feldman. Feldman was a member of the initial cadre that became GSG9.

Admittedly, when Travis and Hans drank beer together after all those Saturday afternoon soccer games, neither could have anticipated the direction their lives would take. For Travis it had changed in 1974 in El Salvador with the shootout defending a local political figure. And for Hans it all took a sharp turn to where he was now, a few years later in 1977 in Mogadishu, Somalia.

Some Palestinian terrorists had hijacked a Lufthansa aircraft named the Landshut. The Landshut was at the time on its way to Frankfurt from Palma de Mallaorca. The terrorists demanded an immediate release of the German Red Army Faction in a sort of ransom for the passengers and crew of the aircraft. This drama continued as the aircraft flew from location to location throughout the Middle East. And during this ordeal the captain of the aircraft, Jurgen Schumann, was murdered while the aircraft was in Aden.

While this drama was playing itself out on the world stage, behind the scenes, powerful forces were in play. The German Chancellor, Helmut Schmidt, and the President of Somalia, Siad Barre, decided jointly that the crisis would be turned over to GSG9 to resolve. Specifically, the GSG9 mission was to storm the plane, rescue the hostages, and end the crisis on terms favorable to Germany and Somalia. With this in mind special envoy Hans-Jurgen Wischenwski and police commander Ulrich Wegner were dispatched to Mogadishu to put the plan in motion.

On about the fourth day of this odyssey, the terrorist hijackers directed the aircraft, a Boeing 737 to fly to Mogadishu where they were supposed to await the arrival of the Red Army Faction members. It seems the German Government had led the hijackers to believe that their demands would be met. In truth, that was the bait to set the trap. As the plan was executed, during the night of 17 October 1977, Somali Ranger units set up a distraction to divert the hijackers' attention, while the members of GSG9 stormed the aircraft.

Seven minutes later, all the hostages were in friendly hands, three of the hijackers were dead, and a fourth was seriously injured. On the friendly side of the operation, one member of GSG9 and one flight attendant had been injured but their injuries were not life threatening, and the 86 hostages were freed. It was a rousing success and an example of what could be done to curb international terrorists who hijack aircraft. Hans Feldman had been a part of that mission and had remained with the unit as committed as he had been on day one of his service with the GSG9.

Old Friends Have Lunch

Hans Feldman and Tavis Lemon sat at a table in the corner of a room at a little out of the way gasthaus frequented by members of GSG9. Hans noted the telltale signs of fatigue on Trav's face, the dark circles under his eyes. He also noticed the tight skin across his forehead where gray hair was starting to emerge at his temples. In a glance, Hans decided his old friend displayed the signs of a man on a quest and showed signs of stress, intense stress. "It has been a while,

Trav, and you look tired. So tell me, were you the target of that incident a few days ago in Istanbul?"

"Yes, it appears I was one of the targets and the other was a young woman with whom I work." Trav answered, then he continued, "But the bigger problem is that they have already eliminated some of my colleagues, and the whole organization is feeling the strain right now. To say they are all stressed out would be a gross understatement."

"And, let me guess," Hans replied, "It is your task to find a solution and, or eliminate the threat. Is that about right?"

"Yep." Was Trav's one word reply.

"So what do you need?" Hans asked bluntly.

"A place to sleep and clean up and think for a day or two." Travis answered.

"Well that part is easy enough. I have an apartment in my home that is not rented right now." Hans offered, "It is yours. What else?"

"I need to find a connection where the IRGC, the Kurds, and the Russians all come together. I think it is likely here in Germany; and I think the 'locus' is likely in Frankfurt."

Hans sat back in his chair and thought a moment, then a mischievous smile crossed his face and he said, "Well, that is easy enough, have you checked the local strip clubs in Frankfurt?"

Travis laughed for the first time in days, "You know, it could be that simple: but somehow I think this might be a little more complicated." Then making a weak attempt at humor himself, Travis said, "Of course, we should go and check out every possibility."

"Better you sleep in, and I will ask a couple of questions tomorrow, you know shake a few trees, and see what begins to emerge." Hans said and then the conversation turned to sports and the light banter of two old friends catching up on life.

On the next morning, following the schnitzels and plenty of late night beer, Travis was sitting with a cup of strong coffee. He was savoring every drop as he gazed out of the huge windows over the valley. He was in the safest place he had seen since leaving his home on the Spanish Costa Brava.

The apartment in which Hans had installed him was really quite nice; and it was secluded near the top of a hill. The only approach by road was one that he could see winding up from the main road below as he sipped his coffee. And even more comforting was that the trails through the woods were also visible from the other side of the room looking out at the forest.

The place itself was set back over a cliff so that any approach from that side would take someone very determined. Hans had handed him a 9mm pistol the night before and had shown him how to start the coffee in the morning. Then he retired to the main house where he lived alone and left Travis with his thoughts. Travis had slept well and he had slept deeply for the first time since leaving Istanbul after the attempt on his life. In fact he had slept late for the first time in as long as he could remember. Then Travis had showered and shaved and dressed in jeans and a casual shirt with the shirttail out to conceal the pistol that was in the waistband of his trousers.

He was relaxing and he liked it; he could see the attraction for Hans to live in this area. Naturally his thoughts wandered to Julie and to hoping she was doing well. She did not like that they could not communicate when he left on his "business trips" but she was still tolerating the situation, at least for now. His reverie was broken by Hans pulling up the road in his gray Mercedes SUV.

Travis opened the door and stood, leaning on the doorframe, as Hans parked the vehicle in a space between his home and this apartment. "Your timing is impeccable. The coffee is on and still hot." Travis called out of the door as Hans exited the vehicle and approached him.

"Sounds good, my friend." Hans replied and then added, "How did you sleep?"

"Better than I have in weeks." Travis responded, "Thank you." Then he stepped aside to allow his host to pass into the little sitting area with the great view out of the large window near the coffee pot.

Hans poured himself a cup of black coffee and they both sat across the table facing each other as Hans took a deep breath and began to speak even before taking his first sip from the mug in front of him. "I had a most interesting couple of hours this morning with our section that does 'Russia watching' for us." Hans said by way of introducing the topic, then he added, "By the way, did you know they are watching you too?"

Travis stopped in the act of raising his coffee cup frozen in mid air like some kind of statue and gave a one-word response, "Really!"

"Ya. Really." Hans replied and then added, "It seems there is one office in particular in Frankfurt which houses the cultural attaché. The incumbent caught their attention because he is starting to dabble in the black market for personal luxuries." Raising his cup he added, "Like American coffee and cigarettes and while it is small scale he could use it like bait to lure in unsuspecting recruits for his dirty tricks in the future. He is relatively new but they had been watching his predecessor quite a while."

"The predecessor?" Travis said, "Sergei Ivanovich? They had been watching Sergei Ivanovich?"

"Ya. You do know that you killed his son, right?" Hans asked.

"Yes, but that was operational in the field and in El Salvador many years ago."

"Well did you know that his son had a best friend at their technical school in Russia? He is a fellow named Farouq and he is now rising quickly in the IRGC, in Iran." Hans added.

"That is interesting." Travis said with the emphasis on the word "is."

And Farouq has a sister, Samira, and that sister has a family that resides here in Germany as permanent residents. And, ever since Sergei met Farouq, as a friend of his son's, he has made routine visits to check on their health and welfare. He also apparently used his political clout, and a physical threat on at least one occasion that we know of, to make sure they had no problems of any kind in Germany." Before Travis could interrupt, Hans added, "And it appears that when his executive secretary, the man named Alfred, who replaced Sergei, sort of 'inherited' the Farouq family as one of his obligations."

"Damn!" Travis said aloud. Then as he continued to put the pieces together in his mind, he asked Hans a most important question. "Where does that leave us?"

"Well, my friend," Hans started, "As you Americans say, 'that is the elephant in the room.' My orders are to stay clear of you; but my orders are also to stay out of your way so as not to interfere."

Travis relaxed and smiled a little as Hans continued, "We have no interest in this situation because no one in the FRG has told us to take action. We are watching because we watch all foreign intelligence initiatives on our sovereign soil. But we do not usually get involved with Allies or their operations unless requested, or if German interests are at stake." Then sipping his coffee he added, "But do try to keep the body count to a minimum if you can. It would be appreciated."

"And what do you have to get from me to take back to your bosses?" Travis asked.

"I need as much as you can tell me." Hans answered evenly.

"Fair enough." Travis said, "Someone is killing off our operatives one by one."

"Was Istanbul a part of that?" Hans interjected,

"Exactly, but we do not know who or why yet. That is my job. I must figure out who and then I must stop them." Travis shared with his old friend. Then the serious conversation began and Hans relayed the information he had been able to gather in such a short time. After about an hour of discussion Travis said his goodbyes and prepared to leave for the next phase that was still forming in his mind.

"Hans, danke fur alles!" Travis said to his old friend as he got into his car.

"Well you can always stay and rest more if you need, Travis." Hans offered but Travis was already shaking his head before the words were out of Hans' mouth.

"You and I both know there is a target on my back and the longer I stay in one place the more I bring danger to old friends like you." Travis responded.

"And what is a little danger between friends," Hans said and then added, "especially for men in our line of work."

"That is true, my friend, but you have enough of your own. And this one is my problem to resolve." Travis said and offered his hand.

Hans looked at the offered hand and said simply, "Oh, you Americans." Then he brushed the hand aside and stepped in to give Trav a huge hug. "This is the way old friends say goodbye and good luck in Germany." Without another word the two warriors parted and Travis drove away.

Checking In

A yellow phone rang on Sheila Makinley's desk and she raised an index finger for quiet as she answered the line with her best "civilian" voice, "Hello." Bob Wallis and his deputy immediately fell quiet despite the fact that the three of them had been in an intense discussion half a second before.

"Darling, I'm so glad I caught you." Sheila motioned for Bob and his associate to pick up the extension earpiece. They did so immediately and heard Travis' next words. "Listen, darling, don't talk just listen please, I do not have much time at all before my train leaves for Frankfurt. I just want to know if I can call you back for a real conversation in about two hours?"

"Yes, of course, darling. I will be waiting, oh and Bob and Fred send their regards. Travel safely dear." And the line went dead.

"Nice." Bob Wallis, Chief of Intelligence said.

"I assume the call will be open to us as well?" Fred Wilson, Bob's deputy, asked.

"Not a field operator type are you Fred?" Sheila asked.

"Well, actually no I am not, I came in from uniformed service with the Army. Why?" Fred replied but there was a little pink around his neck and Sheila knew she had touched a nerve.

"Oh, didn't mean to hit a nerve there, Fred, I know you Army guys get lots of time in the field but this is different." Then Sheila picked up her coffee cup and gave a quick tutorial. "That yellow phone is a mirror of my cell phone and allows me to answer incoming calls without violating the rules by having a cell inside a SCIF area. And it is already set up with additional listening devices so if the line is being monitored an outsider won't hear additional extensions click on as they are being being picked up."

Bob nodded his head in understanding and appreciation as he interjected, "And you always assume the other line is being monitored?"

"Exactly." Sheila confirmed, "That is why neither Travis nor I identified ourselves and the only reason I mention you two was to let him know there would be others on the line when he calls in secure. If he had any problem with that he would have said something innocent like 'give them my regards' but since he said nothing he is expecting to be able to talk freely. And the fact that he called to set it up means he will call back from an encrypted system."

"So where do you want to meet? Back here in your office?" Bob asked.

"Sounds good to me." Sheila confirmed and the session broke up.

Chapter 9: Coordinating

Travis was ten minutes late with the call and the three of them breathed a sigh of relief when the secure phone at the small conference table in Sheila's office chirped. She answered it, "Travis? Is that you?"

"Yes, and we owe a thank you note to the local Commander at this little Kaserne for letting me use his system. I am in a SCIF and I am alone."

"I am here in my office with Robert Wallis, our chief of Intelligence, and Fred Wilson, his deputy, and we are all very interested in what you have to tell us." And with that Sheila and her associates went into the listening and note-taking mode. Thirty minutes later Travis had laid out his travels and consultations thus far, how he had come to return to Germany, and what he saw as a way ahead.

When he came to the end of his narrative there was a moment of silence then Bob spoke. "So, Travis, we have good intelligence now. The Kurdish group in Turkey did set the explosion that almost killed you and Sheila and it was a contract job. The way we see it the tie in is likely this guy Farouq, and of course the fact that he has family in Germany. But Alfred may be calling the shots, am I right so far?"

"That seems to be a viable scenario but there has to be at least tacit acquiescence from Moscow, otherwise nothing would happen."

Travis started but Bob cut him off, "Trav, hold one second. Fred went to the other room to check another system for a minute and he just walked back in, what did you find, Fred?'

"Again it all looks feasible. There is a profile from the Agency on Ivanovich and it goes into some depth with a psychological profile about his fixation on you, Travis. And there is another report on Alfred being implicated in Ivanovich's death in that auto accident. And there is a low level local report, perhaps just a coincidence but I don't believe in coincidences, about a new black-market effort."

Bob continued, "This last tidbit looks like an attempt to smuggle cigarettes and coffee. It involves a low level member of the Russian Diplomatic Service assigned to the Office of the Cultural Attaché in Frankfurt. And finally, there is a police report that Alfred visits an immigrant family from Iran almost as often as Ivanovich visited that same family. But with all of this, they are careful, and there is nothing that tripped any police concerns."

Shifting gears Bob added, "Trav, it may mean nothing, but this guy, Alfred, was caught on an intercept with someone in Dresden and he was getting an ear full. Alfred was telling him about a problem he was having and using some very colorful language. Alfred kept referring to his nemesis by the nickname Vlad. But the only Vlad we can find so far is a Russian internal security guy named Vladimir Putin. This Putin character is an old ex-KGB-guy now doing Stasi-type work. His current activity appears aimed to be aimed at Honecker and his cronies, who are resisting directions from Moscow. Does that help?"

"Yes, it does!" Travis confirmed, "What all of that tells me is that we may be on the right track to finding our enemy." And after the briefest of pauses he added, "And it gives me an idea on how to get at these guys."

"Trav," Sheila spoke up, "I am just looking through this stack of stuff that Fred just brought in to us and I think I know what you are thinking. Tell me if I am right about that. As I look quickly through this stuff there is one thing that jumps out at me. I think the weak spot into Alfred's game may be Svetlana, his new intern."

"You're reading my mind, go ahead please." Travis encouraged.

Sheila continued, "I do not see in her profile any indications or hints that she would be looking to make a little cash on the side with black market coffee. In the Agency profile, she comes across as dedicated to her cause, so I think this is some kind of a game that Alfred put her up to. It is actually quite crafty because this way he can maintain deniability for the Office, and simultaneously he can be fishing to set up American Servicemen willing to do things for profit. That may be an angle you can exploit against him."

"Folks, this all makes a lot of sense and I appreciate the confirmations and corrections as we have been discussing this whole thing." Travis began to wrap up the session and to prepare mentally for the next phase of his operation. With that the call came to an end; but with promises to keep each other abreast of changes when time permitted.

Travis was out of the building and gone within ten minutes. He had given a hearty "thank you" to the Commander and the Command Post Watch Officer, and he had assured them they had just played a big support role to securing US interests in Europe. Then he was back on the move and headed into Frankfurt.

Svetlana

It did not take long to find a good spot to keep an eye on the comings and goings at the building where the Office of the Soviet Cultural Attaché was housed. Travis was siting at a window seat in a coffee shop just down the block and across the street form the building. About midmorning he spotted a twenty-something blonde woman who wore her hair short and her coat hanging open to reveal stylish clothes. Actually she looked no different from the other ladies and what they were wearing on the streets of Frankfurt.

But then Travis noticed something almost without realizing it. His sixth sense kicked in and he realized, now at a conscious level, that there was something in her demeanor that caught his attention. She was a little too attentive and a little too cautious about checking her surroundings. And she looked a little too closely at everyone who approached her, even those who were obviously just passing by, lost in his or her own little world. She did not exactly do anything "wrong" she just did not do enough "right." It was bad tradecraft and looked almost as if it had been learned in a lecture, or perhaps on a video reel, and then the lesson had been left for the student to practice on her own at sometime in the future.

By the time she passed his window he was sure that this was Svetlana, the newly assigned assistant direct from somewhere in Russia. Travis settled his bill at the café and left in the same direction that Svetlana had walked. The difference is he knew that he only needed a glimpse of her once in a while to maintain surveillance. And of course, while there were plenty of blonde German women on the streets most did not walk with the same sense of purpose that Svetlana displayed.

Svetlana turned briskly into an indoor shopping mall of sorts where the stores maintained their street side facades but some enterprising planner had set up an indoor walkway. This was out of the weather and meandered between and among the stores. That way the stores could also maintain a show window and an entrance from the indoor walk. These sorts of shopping areas were becoming popular in the bigger German cities. It was a response of sorts to the huge box stores that had started to appear on the outskirts of town.

Without resorting to driving through streets that were most often wet or icy this time of year, the shoppers of the city could stroll, out of the weather, through the shopping district. Travis wandered idly by the shops lingering at one or another in no apparent pattern to his movements. As he studied her from side glances and from the corner of his eye, he became more and more convinced that she was not here shopping but hunting. It became clear to him that Svetlana was working on her assignment, as Sheila had described it. Svetlana was hunting for a likely target who might be an American or a Canadian "dependent" spouse, and therefore who would have ration card privileges.

Trav's opinion of the young Russian went up a notch. She was hunting in the natural habitat of her prey. She was looking for a military wife, who liked to shop, and therefore might be willing to trade ration card access for money to shop more. And it appeared she had selected a target as she approached a small group of three women joking and laughing as they strolled together. Trav was barely able to hear as Svetlana greeted the other young women and slipped comfortably into their little group. She appeared to know them; Trav just didn't know how well the four might know each other.

Travis managed to snap a picture of the group of four women, Svetlana and her three new friends. Then as if on a stroll he eased quietly past them as they went together into a shop that featured slacks and jackets in the display window. "Well, time to find a coffee shop and watch and wait." He knew that if he followed them further at this time he might as well wave a red flag at a bull. He was pretty sure that none of them had taken note of him yet and he did not want to compromise his surveillance of this little group.

What he needed was a little help setting a trap and he wondered if these women might be willing to be the bait. Travis sipped has coffee and when he saw them leave the shopping area he headed to the US Army Kaserne just outside of town and found the office of the Criminal Investigative Division (CID). His credentials got him immediate access to the Officer in Charge (OIC) and the two were inside a closed room with a couple of the CID Unit's most senior agents.

Fifteen minutes later the four men had a straw man of a plan and an invitation to walk across the compound and brief the Post Commander, again courtesy of Trav's credentials. The Post Commander thanked Travis for the briefing and made one phone call then gave his approval for the operation to continue as a priority due to the US interests involved. An hour later Travis had shared the photographs from his concealable camera and the base photo lab put a rush on the development.

Things Begin To Happen

With the pictures, the CID agents were able to identify the women and locate their husbands who all belonged to the same military unit. With a couple of phone calls the three women and their husbands were assembled at a back room in the CID Office two hours later. The group was confused, surprised and concerned when the CID lead took the floor to speak.

"Good afternoon ladies and gentlemen. I appreciate your willingness to respond on such short notice and I will get right to the point." Sensing the tension building among the small group, the Colonel continued, "First and foremost let me assure each of you that none of you is under suspicion of any misconduct. I apologize for the secrecy but we need your help and you will see the need for that very shortly."

The CID Chief noted that they began to relax a bit as he continued, "Frankly we are asking for your cooperation to conduct a little sting operation that has implications for US Army interests in the local area. So without further delay allow me to introduce Mr. Harry Mellon from another government entity." Then gesturing to Travis he said, "Mr. Mellon the floor is yours."

Travis, now in his Harrison Travis Mellon persona, began softly, "Good afternoon. First let me thank you all for your service to our nation. And, I am afraid, I need to bring you into something that is very sensitive but I will first need you each to sign a non-disclosure statement before we can go any further. I can assure you that this is a grave matter and your help and assistance is very much needed and appreciated."

As Travis spoke, one of the CID agents passed out the papers on clipboards with pens attached. Travis was pleased to see them all sign willingly with minimal hesitation. "Thank you." Trav said as the CID agent collected the clipboards.

The he placed a large 5x8 inch copy of the photo he had taken earlier in the day on the table in front of the room. As the image sank in with everyone Travis continued, "We are not in the practice of observing US

Army soldiers and their families living overseas. But we are in the practice of observing and reporting on known operatives of foreign governments. This is all the more so when these agents are committing or preparing to commit acts that are harmful to the US." He paused a moment for his words to sink in and then continued.

"Ladies, the woman who has been attempting to befriend your little group is named Svetlana. She is here in the FRG under diplomatic cover of the Russian government. And she is assigned to the Office of the Cultural Attaché located here in Frankfurt. To put it mildly, she and her boss are not nice people." There was some uncomfortable shifting of position in the chairs and quick looks around the table among the ladies and their husbands.

One of the husbands, a Captain, spoke up, "Mr. Mellon, surely you can't suspect my wife and her friends of any wrong doing."

Harry Mellon cut him off, "That, Captain, is absolutely correct." There was another collective sigh of relief among the group. Travis gave it a minute and then added, "We think they are being 'groomed' and recruited by a very crafty Russian operative and we want to turn the tables on the Russian and her boss."

"Excuse me," this time it was the Lieutenant on the Captain's left who spoke, "are you wanting to expose our wives to any danger while you and the Russians play your 'spy games'?"

"No, Lieutenant, we are not in the business of exposing Americans to risks for which they did not volunteer. I beg you all to be patient just one more minute while I explain." With that Trav laid out what they anticipated would happen next, as Svetlana looked for someone willing to play in a black market game of cigarettes and coffee. He also told them how this could lead to being pulled into the trap over time for other more sensitive purposes.

Chapter 10: Trap! By Whom, For Whom?

With very little prodding the ladies told how they had first met Svetlana just a couple of weeks before and how she had approached them asking for help. Svetlana had said in obviously accented German, "Entschulendegen sie, connen sie mich helfen?"

They shared how there had been a sort of hesitant response from the group but then Svetlana had then said, "Oh, I am not German either. I am from Austria but my English is pretty good. Shall we speak English?" And there had been a sort of easing of the tension a newcomer almost always brings into the dynamics of a small group.

And within minutes there had been a sort of bond starting to form in this case. The common factor appeared to be a random encounter with someone who also loved to shop and who was as alone in this land as they were. To her credit Svetlana had created a moment where the other women "felt" they had found a kindred spirit.

The Lieutenant's wife had broken the ladies' silence when she blurted out, "That little bitch played us!" She was not the only one showing signs of indignation and irritation and Trav's gut told him these ladies would do what was needed. He briefly sketched a trap of their own. They were asked to go along with Svetlana and lead her to believe they would like some extra money for shopping and expenses.

The group discussion wrapped up with assurances that no violence was anticipated and that there would be commendations for the men and their spouses from the Post Commander when this was brought to a close. They parted company and Travis got back to watching Alfred for kinks in his armor. For Travis, and his propensity to action, this was an agonizingly slow process.

Then as he sat sipping coffee and deciding what his next step might be to unravel this complex and complicated problem everything changed. Trav was seated in what was rapidly becoming his new favorite bar, mainly because of the excellent view of the offices in which Svetlana and Alfred worked, when the bombshell fell. One of the CID agents in civilian clothes passed Trav's outdoor table and dropped a note as he walked by.

Travis deftly picked it up and excused himself to the men's room to see what it said. There were only a few words. "Explosion. Costa Brava. One friendly shot. Call Sheila." Travis returned unhurriedly to the table, finished his coffee and paid the bill and strolled away all the while feeling like he had been hit in the gut.

Explosion On The Costa Brava

The yellow phone on Sheila's desk chirped and she reached for it as Bob Wallis and Fred Wilson both took a deep breath and looked at each other. "Got your message." This was all the voice on the other end of the line said.

"I am very sorry for having to give you this news. First, Julie was shot but she will live and she is getting care and our people are with her." Sheila gave him a second to respond.

"Copy all. Please give her the best care you can find. Anything else?" Travis asked in a cold deadpan voice.

"Yes, there is more to the story and you need the information." Sheila said succinctly.

"Go ahead." The deadpan voice, barely disguising concern, said over the speaker of the yellow phone on Sheila's desk.

"The explosion was set and rigged on a remote detonator," Sheila began, "but the explosion did not harm your special friend. She was hit by a sniper's bullet to her left arm. Clearly the shot was meant to kill her but by the grace of God, or her guardian angel or both, she tripped and fell. That saved her life because the bullet hit her arm instead of her chest. She crawled behind a pile of rubble and hid until we found her. "

"Oh my Lord." Travis said quietly.

"We already had people headed out to check on her and they saw the explosion. So they were on the scene in time to render first aid as she went into shock. Likely that sequence of events threw off the shooter's timing and helped save your lady's life. The sheer coincidence of our man's arrival meant the shooter never got another clear shot." Sheila said quickly and added, "But keep listening carefully, there is more you have to know."

Travis maintained silence on the phone.

"It was all timed so that she would be outside the blast in the house, but that she would be found there near the blast. The analysts and profilers say that was likely a deliberate message to you and to us." Sheila concluded as Bob and Fred finally began to breathe normally again.

"Anything else I need to know?" Travis asked.

"No. Other than to tell you that my heart goes out to her and to you." Sheila said.

"Thank you." And the line went dead as Travis cut the connection.

The next call Travis made was to Hans and as soon as Travis heard Hans' voice he started talking before his old friend could even finish his salutation. "Hey buddy, you better get your head down." Travis said immediately.

And Hans replied, "And why is that?"

"I intend to go operational very soon and there may be some ugly consequences." There was silence for a moment and then Travis continued, "So tell your boss or whoever you have to tell in order to cover your butt and protect yourself. I don't want you to be collateral damage."

"Can I ask why? What changed?" Hans said flatly into the phone.

"They shot my girlfriend. Sniper." Travis said flatly.

"Is she OK?" Hans asked with a note of concern in his voice.

"Yes she is alive and being protected now." Travis responded.

Then in an uncharacteristically cheery voice Hans added, "OK then. Enjoy your hunting trip. Listen, I must go now, I have a pop-up meeting with my supervisor. But I want to hear all about it when you get back. See you then, old friend." And with that both men hung up their phones.

Travis assumed that Hans would tell his supervisor about Trav's visit to his home and how "concerned" he was for the US asset's mental condition and fears that Travis might go "lone wolf." Of course his supervisor would know instinctively that there was much more to the story but he would file the appropriate reports and alert the system. And with bureaucratic efficiency, both Hans and the supervisor would be clear from any fallout having followed due diligence in reporting through the chain of command. They also knew that by the time the report got to anyone who could do anything about it, any action Trav was contemplating, would be complete, and too late for anyone in their chain to affect it.

The Logic Of It All

Travis had no doubt that his old mentor, Aferin Abbas, in Cizre either knew, or had an idea that bad things were about to happen. Like a light bulb going on in his head, he realized this explained his old mentor's reactions when Julie's name had been mentioned. Travis had thought the old man was manifesting his cultural bias that women should bear children, not go to work. But maybe he had been saddened by the thought that Travis might be left with no children if Julie were killed.

But all of that hat, he decided, would be an issue to deal with at a later date. Right now his number one priority was to find who had ordered the explosion and the shot that had been intended to kill Julie. They were most likely the same person. After all someone had called the attack in Turkey that almost took him and Sheila out of the game. Clearly he was as much a target as the other operatives were. Someone wanted all the operatives dead and that would be the person who ordered the attack. It was a crude, almost vindictive, way to smoke him out into the open and watch for him to make a mistake they could exploit.

That link was most likely right here in Germany, and he could feel that he was close to something with Svetlana and Alfred, each for very different reasons, at the Cultural Attache's Office. So yes, he would make a quick trip to Spain just to ensure that Julie was OK, and safe, and to reassure her as much as he could. She had, after all, been shot simply because she knew him. These people he was chasing were animals and deserved to be hunted like animals. And he was going to be the one to find them. He was going on the hunt very, very soon.

Germany was a good place to start the hunt as soon as he could check on Julie and return. There were over 600 thousand "Gastarbeiters" in Germany and of that number, at least 200 thousand were Iranians of one flavor or another. They were mostly centered in and around Frankfurt for a variety of reasons having to do with employment and community. So the Iranians, the Russians and the Kurds were all there; it was time to have someone talk with Svetlana again, soon!

Costa Brava A Short Time Earlier

"Wow!" The spotter said almost with an air of excitement in his voice. "That was well done, and awesome to see!"

"Thank you." The shooter answered, and then added, "That should make the 'lady' happy. It is precisely as she requested." Then he began to break the long rifle into two component parts and put then into a fitted case for transport.

"Heinrich! Wait, she has moved. You did not kill her!" The spotter, Hansel, said quickly.

"Shit!" That was all Heinrich said as he stopped in the act of disassembling the custom sniper rifle, and packing its main components into the travel case. Heinrich quickly put the rifle back into working order and used the powerful scope to scan the target area that he and Hansel had been watching for the past several days off and on. As he scanned he gave a quick narrative, "She has moved, I think behind that pile of rubble but there is a car also there now. And there are two men with weapons out who are giving aid to her."

Then Heinrich put the rifle on its side and turned to look at Hansel, "Hansel, why did you not spot the car arriving. It had to be parking as I took the shot because they are even now on the scene giving first aid?" Why did you not tell me to wait until they had made their check and then passed on. If you had done that then the house would be destroyed and she would be dead and two of the three parts of the contract would be fulfilled." Heinrich over his shoulder, to the spotter. "There is only one more thing to do to fulfill the contract."

The spotter looked at the shooter and said with an edge to his voice, "The car should not have mattered. You should have been more careful with the shot, Heinrich. Do not try to blame me for your bad shot. And, what do you mean three-part contract? What are the three parts?"

The shooter moved his hand, revealing a pistol. The pistol barked twice and the spotter fell and did not move as his eyes clouded over. "Sorry, but Sonja does not like you! Part one was to destroy the house, and part two was to kill the girl, and part three was to kill you. Sonja really does not like you and now I understand why. I will have to find another way to finish the contract. At least you will not be in the way any longer." Then he calmly broke down the custom sniper rifle and put the components in their case for transport as Hansel breathed his last.

Chapter 11: Details Long Distance

Travis called his business in Alicante and Maria answered the phone, "Lemon Import and Export, this is Maria. How can I help you?"

"Maria, this is Travis . . ." Lemon began.

"Oh, Mr. Travis! Es horrible! Senorita Julie has been shot. And your house has been destroyed in an explosion. Are you coming home? What can I do?" Maria was bombarding him with comments and with questions. He listened and waited for her to finish.

"Maria." He said quietly into the phone line.

"Si, senor?" she said as a question.

"I need you to do some things for me, please." Travis said.

"Of course. What is it you need?" Maria answered.

"I am coming to Alicante but I need a place to stay and I need someone to pick me up at the airport and to get me to that place." He paused just a moment, then continued, "And I would like to meet with you as soon as I arrive so perhaps it is best to have someone bring me from the airport to the office. Can you arrange that and then meet me at our office?"

"Yes, sir. That is not a problem." Maria told him.

"Maria, mostly I need to see Julie. Is it possible to talk with her? I have been calling the hospital but they will not connect me." Travis told his assistant.

"Yes, that is correct." Maria said, adding, "The police have a guard at her door and there are some men from your embassy who check everyone entering the room. I have only been able to see her for a moment on one occasion.

"Well, that explains a lot." Travis said and then shifted the subject, "Maria, do you know if my car was also destroyed in the explosion?"

"No, senor Travis, the Jaguar car was at the garage being serviced so it was safe from the damage." Maria said and as he was thinking she added, "You know, it just occurred to me that you could stay here at the business, in the room beside the office upstairs. That is the one you use from time to time to freshen up and prepare for emergency trips. There are even some of

149

your clothes in the closet of that room. I can have a bed moved in before you get here."

"That is a good idea, Maria." She did not need to know that was exactly the solution he had wanted all along and it was good to let her take the credit for the idea. She did not need to know of his stash, in that same room, which included another computer and a couple of weapons. It also contained travel documents under three different names and cash, in a hidden compartment of the room. What he did say aloud to her was, "Can you set me up to talk with the police early the day after I arrive? I think I will be able to get a flight tomorrow, so perhaps the next day with the police. The trip is possible to drive but I do not trust myself to drive that distance right now."

"That is fully understandable. And I will call the police as soon as we hang up from this call. What else can I do?" Maria asked.

"The first priority for me is getting to see Julie. As far as I am concerned, even the police will have to allow for that. And I might need some help if she decides to go someplace more safe for her recovery.

Can you find me some connections in the medical transport business? And," Travis added before she could answer, "do you know if her sister in London has been made aware?"

"Yes. The police contacted the sister, Meredith, when they could not get to you immediately. Meredith is here now. She dropped everything and came immediately. I have talked with her and she is anxious to talk with you as well." Then Maria paused a moment and said in a softer tone, "She said she knows you and Julie were starting to get serious but that you were not legally married and she wants to help, not complicate things here with the authorities."

"Thank you, Maria, she is on my list of people to contact right after we end this conversation. Listen, I know I am asking a lot. Are these thing you can handle?" Travis asked in all sincerity.

"It is no problem, Mr. Travis. Can I make another request for you to consider?" Maria asked almost timidly.

"Of course." Travis responded, "What is it, Maria?"

"We have been getting calls from your friends. You and Miss Julie are very popular and Diego Rivera and his wife, Gretschen, have both called. And as soon as I hung up the phone from their call, Raul and Amalia Osborne called, and so did the Italian fellow Gino Carmine from the resort hotel. And his wife, Anita took the phone from him to express her concern also. I was going to suggest that you close the business for a few days as you sort out everything." Maria said quietly.

Travis only paused a moment before he responded, "No, we do not close for a few days. We close for a month starting tomorrow. Please put up a sign and an electronic notice that we are closed due to an illness in the family, or family emergency, or something like that."

"Yes, I can do this also."

"Good, and please call them all back and ask if we can get together for a private session to talk about what has happened. If her sister comes, I am sure she would like to meet Julie's friends as well."

Maria cut him off and interjected, "Oh, that has already happened. I think all three couples, or at least the ladies have been by her sister's side for the past twenty-four hours."

There was a pause in the conversation and Travis eventually broke it by saying. "Maria, I sincerely appreciate what you are doing right now to help me get through this. If you think of anything else just assume you have my authority to do whatever you need to do, or to spend whatever you need to spend; but let me go and make some more calls. I will let you know more precisely what my plans are by text a little later, if that is alright."

"Of course." Maria said and the line went dead.

Return to Alicante

Maria met Tavis at the airport arriving on the early flight and explained that the hospital would not bend the rules. He would have to wait; he could not see her until ten o'clock when visiting hours started. She drove him to the office where he was pleased to find the private room of the upstairs office had a very acceptable cot and bedding as well as basic toiletries

153

in the little bathroom. It was tight but it had a shower and the other essentials.

He dropped his bags and went back to the outer office where she was waiting. Travis and Maria sat and talked through the status of things. He explained that he would like to drive out to the remains of his house just to look things over, even if it might only be to view the damage from a distance because of the police presence. He knew that would also occupy some of the time until the hospital would allow him to visit Julie at 10:00 AM when normal visiting hours started.

Julie's sister, Meredith, was in from England, and that was a good thing. Travis would see her at the hospital and he was a little concerned about her reaction. He had only seen her a few times before, and that had been under much better circumstances. He needed to let her know that, tomorrow morning he would meet with the police.

With that basic coordination resolved, Travis asked Maria about his car. She told him that the mechanic had insisted on holding it until Trav returned. Travis told Maria that the status of the car was fine, and he would like to walk the distance to clear his head, to get to the mechanic's place of business. He and Maria said goodbye temporarily and Travis left for his stroll.

Fifteen minutes later he was talking quietly with the owner and operator of the garage. The owner was a man named Charles Bissell, a retired British Special Air Service (SAS) member, and someone whose ancestors had originally come from this area. Charles had re-adopted the Spanish version of his name, which was Carlos.

According to the sign out front, Carlos Bissell owned the best mechanic garage in the area. In truth it was also the best garage anywhere in the surrounding provinces. He and Travis had met when Trav had first come to the area and had become very good, very quiet friends.

Carlos saw him coming and went to greet him and usher him into his private office. "Trav, I am so sorry to hear. I assume this has a relation to the business you and I are no longer involved in?" It was a question.

Travis answered it honestly, "I do not now, but I fear that is exactly the case, and Julie was almost killed because she was too close to me and in the wrong place at the wrong time. And I want very much to get my hands on those people but first I have to go through a few formalities. Carlos, Julie is very, very special to me." And for the first time Travis let a tear escape his eyes.

"Well, old man," I thought you might feel that way. I took the liberty of making a few modifications to the old Jag, my gift to you just in case." Then the former SAS man winked.

"And exactly what did you do to my car?" Travis asked.

"Let's just say that your mileage may suffer a bit, but the engine will produce even more power and faster acceleration than before. Oh, and that little compartment, that you had hidden, beside the driver's right thigh, in the center console, is exactly the right size for a 9mm pistol and a couple of spare clips. Then

I added a spare oil tank underneath with several gallons of oil. The switch to spray the road behind you is under the dash. I will show you exactly where in a minute." Carlos said smiling.

"And, is that all?" Travis teased him.

"Well, walk over here a moment and open the trunk." Travis followed Carlos and opened the trunk of the car. Carlos continued talking and pointing, "You see right here, inside the trunk, when you raise the lid; now look to the top and there is a little release right here. That device will enable a shelf of sorts to fall down from the trunk lid, like this."

Carlos activated the little switch and the shelf dropped open on its hinges. And they were looking at a Turkish made shotgun, an AK-47 rifle, several throwing knives and half a dozen grenades. Each piece was fitted into cutouts in the lining so nothing would rattle around and or explode inconveniently on its own. Travis just stood there in admiration as Carlos took a breath and added, "This is all off the books of course but if you don't need the gear I would like it back when you finish."

"Carlos, I sincerely appreciate this." Travis said and shook the man's hand.

"Trav, I just wish I could have done more but time and supplies were in short supply."

They shook hands again as Travis slid into the driver's seat and drove back to his office to pick up Maria. Then they rode together out to his property to see what they could see. They had just enough time before the hospital would allow him to visit Julie.

What Maria and Travis saw was horrific! The remains of the building were mostly a black charred mass of twisted metal, broken wood and building materials. The police had a man there who asked their business and then expressed his sorrow to Travis and Maria on the loss of his villa and the attack on his partner. But the man said they could not walk around in the site at this time. Travis informed him they would meet with the inspectors tomorrow and would ask for permission then.

Following that depressing stop, Maria and Travis drove in a kind of uneasy silence as they headed to the hospital to meet Meredith and visit with Julie. They parked the jaguar in visitor parking and made their way to the hospital entrance with ten minutes to spare. They were met by someone who escorted the little entourage to Julie's floor and then to her room.

Travis was very pleased to see the police screening visitors and checking identification. He was even more pleased to see someone from Tango Section beside the policeman conducting his own screening operation. Travis nodded at the fellow whom he recognized from weapons qualification courses. Periodically the Embassy security, and US Marines assigned to the Embassy, used a shooting range outside of Madrid to keep their skills sharp. The fellow nodded back and smiled ever so slightly at Travis.

Chapter 12: Details In Person

The hospital staff had put Julie in a very large room that actually had another bed, but the second bed was unused, and some extra sitting chairs had been arrayed around her bed. Travis realized immediately this was a direct result of the Embassy interest into the destruction of the villa and the attack on Julie. Travis had arrived just as the doctor was finishing his visit with Julie, doubtless this was a part of his morning rounds and he took a moment to greet Travis and then Meredith who had just arrived as well.

"All things considered, the lady was very lucky." The doctor began. Her wound was from a high velocity weapon but the bullet passed through the tissue of the upper arm and 'gracias a Dios' did not hit any of the bones in the upper arm. There will be some minor scaring but the patient," he smiled at Julie, "will recover full use of the arm and the muscle tissue will repair itself in time."

"Thank God!" Meredith said aloud.

"Yes. Exactly." The doctor agreed and then, turning to Travis and looking from him to Julie, he added, "I understand that the police are concerned with the nature of the assault and the possibility of securing the patient's security in the future. This is really their area of expertise and not mine but, let me say, that as a practical matter, she will need time and quiet to fully recover both physically and emotionally. What I am trying to say is please get her someplace quiet and safe for a while where she can deal with the mental issues that such attacks often bring."

The doctor let his words sink in and then added almost brusquely, "And now if you will excuse me I must take care of a few details for some of my other patients." Then he said his goodbyes. As he left the room, Travis asked the two guards to close the door behind the doctor so the three of them could have a little privacy.

There was a moment of silence then Julie spoke for the first time, "Trav, just hold me a moment." Travis stepped forward leaning over the side of her bed and did as Julie requested being careful not to get anywhere near her bandages. Julie let herself cry a moment then gently pushed Travis away to be replaced by her sister, Meredith. The two women comforted each other for several moments then the two of them stood closely around Julie's hospital bed.

A Time For Truth

Travis knew intuitively that the shooter had been a pro. The wound was in her left arm not too far from the elbow, which means she had fallen to the right and that had saved her life. The shooter had intended a shot to the heart but her fall pulled her out of harm's way and the bullet passed through her arm instead of her chest. This was what he thought but what he said was, "Julie, there is something you need to know."

Julie looked at Meredith and the two of them shared some unspoken communication. Meredith broke the silence, "I think we know already and I think that Julie is coming to London with me were I can watch over her because you will be gone again tomorrow, is that about right, Travis?"

For the first time in his adult life Travis was literally without words as he ran the mental gymnastics to fully take in what was happening. Then it all connected and he said simply, "You two already know, don't you?"

Julie gave a little laugh then grabbed her shoulder as the motion of laughing had obviously made the wound hurt. "Travis, we are not idiots." And she gave him a warm smile.

"Besides," Meredith added, "I saw you in your swim trunks without a shirt last year and you have enough scars for a whole rugby team. And, I might add, you are a little too fit for a businessman your age."

"And," Julie took up the theme, "Travis, I work for the airlines and I am all over the airports, here and Madrid and the other airports we support, all the time. I have seen that fellow you introduced to me, as Mr. Smith, a few years ago, and his assistant, Miss Barclay leaving or arriving on international flights out of Madrid numerous times. She is always seeing him off or welcoming him back, but his name changes from time to time and hers does not. Oh and they always have an embassy car waiting at the curb outside."

Then Julie and Meredith looked at each other again and Meredith took over again. "Travis, you don't have to say anything really. Julie is coming home with me to London as soon as they will clear her to leave the hospital and fly. And you should not worry because my husband's uncle, the Brigadier, has some pals in the SAS who will be staying close and keeping an eye on things out in the country. We are taking Julie to my husband's old family place outside of the city and away from prying eyes. You can come collect her when you finish."

Julie cut in again, "Now, go find the bastards who did this and make sure they never get to do anything like this again." As she said the last word she squeezed Trav's hand and smiled in that way that almost melted his heart.

There was another moment of silence and then Travis confirmed everything without saying so. What he did say is, "I promise you that they will never do this again to anyone, and yes, I do have to go. But I think I have to see the police first."

"Oh, one more thing." Meredith said as Julie and Trav looked into each other's eyes. The two of them broke the gaze and looked over to her and she continued. "Just one more piece of advice, Travis, when this is all over and you come to collect Julie, bring a ring with you."

"Meredith!" Julie said loudly.

"Actually," Travis responded, "I was just thinking the same thing. A woman this smart and beautiful should not be loose and 'blowing in the wind,' so to speak. She needs to be tied down to a quiet married life."

"Exactly!" Meredith answered.

"Travis, are you proposing?" Julie said.

Travis dropped to one knee beside the bed but never let go of her hand, "I am indeed asking for your hand in marriage. Will you make me the happiest man in the world?"

"Oh, my God!" Julie said.

"Is that a yes?" Travis asked.

"Yes." Julie said pulling on his hand. "A thousand times, yes."

Travis responded to the tug on his hand and stood smoothly to lean over the bed to hug and kiss her tenderly. "By the way," Travis said, "I may need to relocate when this is over. How do you feel about Italy? Maybe Naples? Or, along the Amalfi Coast someplace?"

Julie did not get a chance to answer as Meredith interjected herself more forcefully this time. "Like I said," Meredith started with a smile in her voice, "bring a ring! Just remember those SAS chaps and the Brigadier. They take these things very seriously!"

"I shall indeed." Travis said looking from Julie to Meredith and back.

But the moment was interrupted by a commotion at the door and the three of them looked over to watch an unsuccessful attempt by the police, and the embassy man, trying to keep Gretschen Rivera, Amalia Osborne, and Anita Carmine from entering the room. Travis relieved the tension by crossing to the two men and explaining that the ladies were best friends. And if they could please be allowed to visit Julie and Meredith, then he could keep his appointment with the Police Inspector downtown. As he left, Julie was making introductions and Meredith and the ladies were getting acquainted. Julie shot him one more glance and a smile, but he doubted the others even saw him leave.

With The Police

Travis spent a frustrating couple of hours with the police but he knew he could not rush their process. It was frustrating because he and the police wanted the same thing. He wanted to get whatever data he could from them and to answer their questions without giving away too much information himself. And they wanted as much information as they could get from him about who might do such a thing, without giving up whatever their investigation might be able to uncover.

After asking about any illegal activities that he or Julie might have been involved in, and about the specific nature of their relationship, they turned to Trav's business activities. Here Travis was able to regain some degree of control because he invited them to come by and have a look at his books and his business activity. He also said that his business manager, Maria, would be more than willing to host them. And, no he would not be staying here the next few days because he needed to finish his business trip, but he would be returning as soon as that was completed. It was toward the end of this particular session that the lawyer arrived from the US Embassy.

The lawyer assured the police that Mr. Lemon was not "running" just returning to his work. And the lawyer mentioned how important this "work" was to the US interests in Spain and to the rest of southern Europe. He also assured them that neither Travis nor Julie were involved in any illegal activity. And he presented them with a document advising them that Julie would travel with her sister on a special medical transport. Her family was bringing her home to England in order for her to recover from her injury and wound. And, surely that would assure her safety without requiring any of their already limited resources.

The lawyer also explained to the police that Mr. Lemon had served as an ex-US Military Officer with distinguished service as well as being a former US Government Service civilian employee. In fact he was known to the Spanish military through his import and export company. He was also known to the Guardia Civil and trusted by them to handle the import of some of their equipment.

The lawyer also hinted that Travis might have worked counter terror issues in the past. So it was possible that this whole thing might well be some sort of retribution from those days. But, he assured them, neither the Embassy nor Mr. Lemon had anything concrete, and for that matter, they collectively had no idea exactly who or why such a thing might have been done. Again he re-emphasized that Travis needed to leave the local area to return to his business trip, specifically to Germany, but that would be there for a short time only.

The lawyer repeatedly made the point that Mr. Lemon had substantial business interests in the area and that he provided jobs to local people. He also had an active social life, which included other business men and social leaders. Then the lawyer pointed out that Travis and Julie regularly entertained local people like Diego Rivera and his wife Gretschen, as well as Raul and Amalia Osborne. And the circle of friends included Gino and Anita Carmine as well as informal friends from work. Clearly, the lawyer argued he had social, emotional and business ties to the area and definitely he was not planning to leave Europe.

With the assurances from the lawyer and from Travis himself, and a few phone calls to the Riveras, the Osbornes and the Carmines, the senior police official determined that Travis was not a "flight risk." He was released and encouraged to return as soon as he could complete his business outside of Spain. Finally, in response to a formal request from the lawyer for any details they could share, the Police told of another body in the area where they had been looking for evidence of the shooter. The fellow was Russian and a career criminal but the bullet that had wounded Julie was from a high-powered sniper rifle. And the Russian criminal had been killed by a large caliber handgun at close range. The two events were not thought to be directly related.

Trav's first thought was, "Bullshit! They are definitely related." But all he said was, "How odd." At least that was all he said to the police. He did place a call to his friend Hans to let him know he was headed back to Germany and would like to talk with him again. He also told Hans that he may have something of interest. Then he assured his old friend that he would not be asking for anything, but he might have stumbled on to something and he wanted to "share." But he had to check in with his people first and that meant a quick trip to Madrid to consult with Tango Section Field HQ. Travis called Sheila's direct number and made plans for a quick in person chat.

Chapter 13: The Yellow Desk Phone Rings

"This is Sheila." The well-dressed, and slightly harried looking, woman said into the yellow phone on her desk and the rest of the room went quiet. Everyone else in the room froze in mid air as they watched and listened. They watched their boss, Sheila Makinley, as she listened to the voice on the other end before responding, "Yes it would be great to get together. Can you come to me?" Sheila waited just a moment and ended the call saying, "Great, I look forward to seeing see you then."

Turning to face the room full of eyes and ears focused on her expectantly. It was like an orchestra gazing intently at the conductor who had just tapped the music stand with the baton. Sheila said simply, "Tomorrow morning at about 0900, in the SCIF Travis will be here. Gather up all the bits and pieces we have, including the attempts last night on our team in Azerbaijan." As if on cue everyone started working a computer keyboard or reaching into a file drawer or heading off down the hall as if on an urgent task. And, in truth, they were all on an urgent task.

The principals and their subordinates would work late tonight but some of their subordinates would work all night long. Everything would be set for a pre-brief discussion with the morning coffee when the principals came back to the embassy. But no one complained; this is what they lived for. Sheila, Bob and the rest of the team might not be out in the field but, collectively they all served as a nerve center. They were the central clearing house for the info that the Tango Section operators needed to be effective. Everyone knew it was a contest that could mean life or death and right now they were under attack. This was about survival!

Back In Frankfurt

In fact, in the interim while Travis was busy in Spain, time had not stood still for Sheila and Bob. In fact one of their younger colleagues, a psychologist by academic training, who already knew where Svetlana lived, had waited outside her apartment. When Svetlana was seen leaving in the direction of the building that housed the Office of the Cultural Attaché, things kicked into a higher gear. Their young colleague had quietly and quickly crossed the street and entered the building where Svetlana lived. It was not hard to enter the building with the morning activity on the sidewalk and the frequently open front doorways of the residential apartment buildings.

A young operative, the psychologist, was as they say, hiding in plain sight, and going unnoticed. Entering the front door had been so simple as to be laughable. All that breach took was a flirtatious smile, and an older gentleman who was leaving even held the door for her to enter. When she arrived at the door of Svetlana's apartment she promptly picked the lock.

This was almost as fast as using a key; and the lock was no challenge at all. Once inside, she could take her time methodically picking apart every aspect of Svetlana's life here in Germany. After the first hour the psychologist took a cell phone from her pocket and called a yellow phone located hundreds of miles away in Madrid. It was answered immediately.

"This is Sheila." The voice said.

And the young woman said simply, "This is Janet, and I am at the shop." Janet waited a second for any new instructions that might come from her superior, but there was only a couple of seconds of silence. Janet used even that time to continue scanning the apartment with the practiced eye of someone who lives by her wits and instincts.

Finally the voice from the yellow phone said, "Happy shopping, dear." Then the phone line went silent. Even as Janet put it back into her pocket, she was continuing a methodical search of Svetlana's personal effects.

Even so, and not surprisingly, Janet learned the most from the photos and letters she ran across in the apartment. More to the point she learned from what was not present in the apartment. From what she could see, it all verified the theoretical profile from Bob Wallis and his people.

Svetlana appeared to have grown up as an orphan in an institution. The only pictures were with other equally lonely looking girls in some sort of cold clinical setting. The backgrounds were mostly devoid of pictures on the walls and in rooms with almost no furniture.

Janet, the psychologist, was not naïve and knew this could all have been an engineered setting to put people like her onto a wrong path but somehow she didn't think so this time. There were only a few pictures and only a few letters and they had surprisingly bad handwriting. And what she could make out from the content, the writing was not very polished.

There was no sign of a boyfriend, or for that matter a girlfriend either. Janet knew that Svetlana lived alone from the previous surveillance but she saw no tell tale signs of another presence. She did find a couple of romance novels, a TV and a radio tuned to a classical station. Nearby on a shelf she did find some academic books regarding Communism and the construction of a Socialist economic state. So she could surmise that Svetlana had either been a serious student or wanted others to surmise that she was a serious student of the Communist ideal.

It was not long before the incongruence of this setting hit the psychologist in the face like a cold gust of air on a wintery morning. What Janet was seeing was at once consistent and inconsistent with her first impressions. The lady's makeup for example was all very expensive and all with French labels.

And her shoes were all Italian, based on the labels, and equally expensive. Additionally, her wardrobe may have been modest in the sheer number of items of clothing, but every piece Janet could see was well maintained and showed signs of tailoring. That would have given the clothes the look of a "perfect fit" that she had seen in Svetlana's daily appearance.

"So," she reasoned with herself, "Svetlana is a snobbish socialist who likes to look nice. Or she is a poor orphan who is discovering the good life in the western capitalist world." This gave Janet pause to revisit the small writing table and nightstand again. This time she looked a little more closely and she found some magazines she had overlooked before.

She knew that her colleagues in Virginia would have said to focus on the books since people do not normally find their political inspiration from glossy magazines. But she also knew that people did explore their interests through magazines without getting "attached" as they might to a book. This was especially so in the USSR where books were pretty well edited and controlled by the propaganda machine. And they were expensive so people chose them with some thought.

This time as she went through the magazines, Janet took note of the pages that had been dog-eared. The pages with the corners folded over might be revisited; and she found a theme begin to emerge. The most revisited images seemed to be of Italian beaches, Parisian cafes, and German houses being decorated or redecorated. The psychologist began to smile as it all sank in; and an approach for interrogation began to form in her conscious mind.

It was an extension of the one that had been peeking out through the folds of her subconscious mind as she had gone through the apartment. This woman, Svetlana, was due for an existential crisis in her future as she came to grips with whether she was a true communist socialist or not. Janet knew this could be exploited as Svetlana came to realize consciously that she was really a captive of a corrupt and ineffective system.

The former possibility would put her on a path to be a really dangerous opponent at some time in the future as a true believer. And the other option would put her on a path to defect and become a convert to the western values and lifestyle. Janet was going to expedite that crisis and offer Svetlana some options.

This was an esoteric conundrum for Janet, so she did what she always did; she went with her instincts in the field. All of that meant she would sit quietly and make herself a cup of tea and wait for Svetlana to return home. Janet sat and sipped her tea and worked through the possible outcomes in his mind. And of course, the first thing she needed was to get a little muscle in here as a backup. Janet put down the teacup and reached for the cell phone in her pocket again.

Svetlana Returns Home

Svetlana had left work at her usual time and made the relatively short commute to her apartment in the usual amount of time. She stopped at the corner store with its kiosk and picked up a few things for her evening meal. And the whole time she kept reflecting on what an ass her boss was.

And that fellow who kept calling from Dresden, Vlad, was another rude Russian. He and Alfred were clearly, in her opinion, members of the apparatchik who were now becoming more and more prevalent within the party infrastructure. They all spouted the noble sounding words of Marx but it only took a moment to realize they would knife each other in the back, in a heartbeat. What was the American saying she had heard in her technical training school; be careful around the elephants because you can get crushed even when they are making love.

She had known Alfred long enough to realize that he was a true believer but not in the Communist Ideal. He was a true believer in setting up his own personal future within that party. Well, OK, if she were totally honest she was also interested in her own future too. She could already see that joining the youth party had been a good move. It had gotten here out of the orphanage and into a technical school and here she was, just a few years later, quickly becoming a "trusted member" of the diplomatic community in West Germany.

Who would have ever thought that poor little Svetlana, who had to drop to her knees and suck the headmaster, would be a diplomat!   But she had survived in the orphanage and now here she was, in Western Europe wearing well-made clothes all tailored for her figure. And these Italian shoes felt so good, even at the end of the day, they were to die for.

Nothing in Russia came close to the workmanship, the style, or the comfort. And, they showed off her legs to good effect. She knew she would bide her time, do whatever the little shit she worked for required. And now that he had forced himself into their office world she would stay on Vladimir's good side, if he had one, and she would look look for her opportunity. Svetlana would find a way to get the hell out of Russia and the Soviet Union forever.

"Maybe," she fantasized, "someday I will find a way to get Maritza out of Russia as well."   That brought a single tear to her eye as she remembered the way the two young girls had comforted each other sleeping in the same bed. They had not done anything sexual really, just held and comforted each other through those insanely cold winters. And it had been Maritza who had figured out how to get the headmaster to give them a few extra tings like a better blanket and a little more food.

She had even toyed with offering the same favors to Alfred but she wasn't sure he would not turn her in for being corrupt and mark her record in some way. No, better to stay distant and professional with that jackass. Besides, she wasn't sure he even had a cock in the first place. He weaseled his way in on every project he could find in order to look as good as possible. And she had learned that he maintained the contacts left behind by his predecessor. But he did not seem to be developing and nurturing new contacts. Oh well, what did she know; besides she just wanted this as a portal to a better life.

This is where her thoughts were, as she absent-mindedly inserted the key and opened the door to her apartment. She caught the vague scent of a strange perfume and then everything went black. She came back to consciousness in this world tied securely to a chair. There was a pounding in her head and as her vision cleared she could see a well-dressed young woman sitting across from her sipping a cup of tea. Then she noticed the very fit looking young man in the room who was standing nearby and apparently waiting for orders.

Svetlana tried to scream but there was something stuffed in her mouth effectively gaging her. She tried to move but her hands were secured behind her back and her legs were each secured at the ankle to a leg of the chair. She also saw that the athletic man was holding a gun hanging down from is side in his right hand. It was clearly a weapon but the barrel flared and she realized there was likely a silencer incorporated into the barrel.

So, her head hurt but she was unharmed as far as she could tell. Her clothes were so far in tact but her head did not just hurt, it throbbed. Her attacker held a "professional" weapon and seemed calm as he waited and the woman sipped her beverage. Svetlana did what she could do; she looked at him and at her and grunted to get their attention.

The psychologist saw realization sink in as the woman's face took on a quizzical and questioning expression. She was asking for information. "Well," Janet thought, "that's a good start." But she said nothing for a moment as she took the last sip of tea. Then she leaned forward with her elbows on her knees, and spoke to Svetlana in German.

Getting To Know Each Other

Svetlana focused as the woman who appeared to be in charge started speaking German to her. German? So was she American, or German, or maybe even Russian? The German was "haut Deutsch," or high German, so she was well educated and the accent was excellent. Wait a minute, what had she said? The fellow with the gun would remove the gag and give her something to counter the effects of the chloroform.

So that was what they had used to knock her out as she had entered the apartment. And now, they wanted to talk. That was good; Svetlana had feared she would be tortured, abused and killed. Immediately she began to relax just a bit and to calm her nerves and her fears.

The woman was repeating the same information but this time in English. "Yes." Svetlana nodded her head. She understood and the demands so far seemed reasonable. Svetlana was now sure this was not some kind of a test from the KGB to new field agents. She was sure of this because those brutes, her countrymen, were not so focused nor were they so considerate. So the woman in charge had to be American or German and she was guessing American. In fact both the young woman and the muscle man were too well dressed to be Russian.

Svetlana nodded her understanding and settled down, getting as close as she could come to being calm. The man leaned over and removed the gag from her mouth. Then he freed her hands behind her back and held out a pill and a glass of water after laying the weapon on the table at his side. "Thank you." She said simply and then added, "What is it you want of me?"

"Information." The woman said simply. She waited a moment longer and let Svetlana swallow then offered her more water. Svetlana nodded and the man held the glass as she took another swallow.

"Thank you." Svetlana said again but this time she added, "Yes, we can talk. But, first I must go and pee."

"Go ahead." Janet said with a deadpan expression.

"Are you insane?" Svetlana said raising her voice, and the young man found himself cracking a smile as Svetlana continued, "Look, this skirt cost a small fortune! Talking is easy and even a little bruising, you might do, will heal. But good clothes, custom tailored, are just too dear."

The fire and the indignation in her eyes were real as she continued, "And I did not mention the potential to damage these shoes. These are Italian! Do you realize how hard it is to find nice shoes these days?" Then huffing in frustration Svetlana added, "Of course you do realize. You are a woman after all!"

Janet found himself starting to like this woman as Svetlana continued, "I do really have to go, so please just untie my ankles so I can pull this skirt up so I can relieve myself without ruining my clothes, please."

The psychologist nodded and the young man took out a pocketknife with his other hand and cut the bonds to release her ankles. He then put the knife away, handed the weapon to Janet and helped Svetlana stand and steady herself. He turned her around and walked with her arm in his left hand as he steered her to the little bathroom. When she started to close the door he put his foot in the way and shook his head, "The door stays open. Try anything heroic and it will be your last action."

Svetlana nodded understanding and almost a little shyly she pulled her skirt up, her panties down and sat on the toilet. As she wiped herself she glared at him, then stood and rearranged her clothes, he said, "I do apologize for the invasion of personal privacy, but it was necessary."

"Humph." Was all Svetlana said in reply. Then she washed her hands and turned to ask, "Now what?"

"Now we talk." The man took her arm again and led her back to the table indicating she should sit but this time he did not restrain her. Clearly the woman in charge had already decided which tact to take based on her appreciation of the finer things of life that Svetlana was enjoying here in the FRG.

Sheila And Bob In Madrid

The "must do" actions in Spain to take care of Julie's needs might have understandably slowed Travis, but it had not derailed him. The delay had been necessary to protect his cover and identity for future operations. More importantly, it had been necessary to make sure Julie was taken care of so he could focus on the tasks ahead. With her sister, Meredith, on hand to watch over Julie, Travis had excused himself and headed to Madrid to get his head back in the game.

As Sheila prepared for Trav's visit and briefing, she reminded herself, that if they did not find the key to all of this quickly it would be a disaster. Tango Section would not have enough field operatives to remain effective at their little niche wars. These were the actions that fell outside of military special operations activities. Besides, other government agencies had more visibility; and therefore, they had more visible government oversight.

Everyone knew how they had all gotten to this point and everyone collectively lamented the situation. They also understood it had been politically unavoidable at the time and had been done for all the right reasons. The Carter Administration had crafted a course of action that, for financial reasons, based on the national economy of the time, had moved resources around in the government.

They had reallocated the funds from an extensive human intelligence network to very high tech electronic intelligence capabilities. In the subsequent months there had been budget cuts and restructuring of federal agencies. In that merciless, and sometimes asinine, process an obscure section of one of these bureaus had survived in part because it was so small by federal standards it was almost invisible.

In the government hierarchy there were bureaus and agencies under secretary level oversight and control. These were then divided into offices, and directorates, and departments, and eventually down to sections. The people in Tango Section at the time had a little inside joke about the name.

The military uses the designation "tango" in their phonetic alphabet to designate "target." So the insiders referred to their organization as "Tango Section" in part because it had survived the targeted cuts to intelligence operations. It also seemed to always be involved in those situations that required a low-level hands-on approach with deniability at the upper levels of the National Security apparatus. They ran the "target section" now known as Tango Section.

Early the next morning, after the call on the yellow desk phone, Sheila Makinley was sitting at the head of a table in a secure briefing facility. She was bringing together the available intelligence on a very serious threat. They were scrambling to prepare their best option for success in ending this nightmare. That option was Charles Travis Lemon, Operative #5 of Tango Section.

If he failed, more people would die and their function in the government would likely be subsumed by one of the other organizations. The problem with that is those other organizations were like using a hammer, or in the case of the military, a sledge hammer, when a smaller effective tack hammer was called for. Therefore, as they were fond of saying, failure was not an option!

The Briefing Back In Madrid

Travis came into the room as they were assembling the final bits of data and turned immediately to Sheila. "Good morning, I cannot tell you how much I appreciate the effort on such short notice and the opportunity to share data. I also apologize for the rushed nature of this, I must be on a flight back to Alicante in a few hours and then a long road trip this afternoon late. I intend to start operations in the target area this week, in fact within two to three days."

That got a few raised eyebrows but it also focused the energy in the room to making him as ready as he could be to understand the landscape against which he had to work. And it was way beyond complicated! This group of professionals might have occasional bureaucratic disagreements but when it came to the bottom-line they all understood the one goal and the one objective to make the Nation stronger. In this case it was even more personal because the enemy had literally been killing them one at a time.

Travis outlined his trip to Cizre, in more detail this time, and finished with what he had learned from the police here in Spain. He also recapped his own visit to the scene of the attack on Julie at the site where his home was now a pile of rubble. By the end of the first hour a better image of the threat began to emerge.

Here the "ints" began to earn their money because they had communications intercepts and banking documents and images that appeared barely connected when taken alone. But they were fitting in as missing pieces of the puzzle as the team continued working together. This had always been one of the strengths of Tango Section; specifically, there was a history of close integration between on the ground expertise and the best high tech information that could be developed. No one could deny the synergies this cooperation developed.

The leadership of this threat seemed to reside somewhere between Alfred Jakovich in Frankfurt, and Farouq the IRGC Iranian, and whoever the hell this guy Vladimir Putin was in Dresden. Then there was the re-emergence of Sonja who was acting almost like a field operations deputy calling the shots on the ground. The team, here assembled, was also very interested in the long-term potential of Svetlana as a sleeper for future exploitation by their organization.

At the end of the session with all the loose ends and unanswered questions not withstanding, Sheila asked the hard question. "Trav, what is your gut level estimate of the body count so we can get ahead of the fallout?"

Without bating an eye, Travis said, "Somewhere between six and twelve depending on the resistance I run into."

"Then we will hope you have a successful operation with very little resistance. But we will also have some backup and some clean-up teams ready to go." Sheila replied.

The group broke up in time for Travis to make his flight connection and the group had more time to talk among themselves after he had gone. What became abundantly clear was that there was no other option. With the death of Johnson and Kinderson followed by the attack on Sheila and Trav in Turkey everyone knew this was someone trying to take the section down in a very permanent way. And of course with the escalation to the destruction of Trav's home and the wounding of his lover in Spain, this all became much more personal. Every one could relate to the idea of someone coming after your family members and loved ones. And of course the attack yesterday on their team in Azerbaijan just reminded everyone that they were deadly serious.

So everyone committed himself or herself to their individual expertise and reached out to see what the environment was like that Travis was walking into. They would make every attempt to warn him of danger and to mitigate any damage he might cause as he resolved this crisis. Sheila also hoped they were all correct in agreeing to go after this threat; meaning she prayed they had the correct target.

They all knew that Russia was a ruthless adversary. And among them the quip was that Russia was not so much a political entity as organized crime masquerading as a nation state. The Soviets were just so damned good at using surrogates and deniable actions and casting doubt on everything. And they were masters of misdirection to the extent that sometimes one agency inside Russia might be working in direct opposition to another agency which only served to cast doubt and confusion on what they were really doing.

Sheila remembered an analyst who once made the point that dealing with Russia and Russians was like playing chess against them. In any world class tournament the Russians always had three or four players to every chess master from another country. As soon as any of the Russian players beat one of the foreigners, the other Russian competitors would lose to the triumphant Russian. In other words the other nation had to beat every one of the Russians; but the first Russian to win against the foreigner could count on scoring a win against all of his or her Russian teammates.

Meanwhile Travis sat on his flight back to Alicante running a mental checklist. Travis, through Maria, knew that Meredith and Julie had gotten safely aboard the medical airlift that had been arranged. Maria put out the word that the business was closed due to an unspecified "family emergency." Then with the knowledge and assurances that Julie was safe in the UK with family and friends, Travis said goodbye to Maria. He grabbed his "go bag" from its hiding place in the room above his office and put it into the trunk of the recently "modified" Jaguar. Now, he was ready to start the drive north to Germany, and off the grid.

Driving would be physically grueling but it would also lower his footprint. He would not risk being spotted in person or electronically going through an airport. And he would have his backup gear in the car, thanks to Carlos Bissell. And if push came to shove he could go completely off the grid and just sleep in his car.

Travis drove up the coast out of Alicante and by the time he passed the outcropping of rock that was home to the Peniscola Castle he could feel the difference in performance in the car. "Thank you, Carlos." He said to no one but he also made a little pledge to give the old SAS guy a case of really good wine. He had already checked out the "modifications" and was pleased with the variety of weapons and capabilities Carlos had added to his vehicle.

The sun was setting as he passed the Abbey of Montserrat and headed north across the border with France. Under other conditions he might well have stopped someplace in Avignon and get some rest but tonight. But the home of the Palais des Papes would not see him tonight.

He did permit himself a smile as he recalled the time he and Julie had spent in this place on holiday, a couple of years ago. Tonight he would press on north toward the border with Germany and he would not take a real break until he crossed that border. The whole trip was about a thousand miles and except for rest stops for bathroom and coffee and maybe a sandwich he was moving as fast as he could.

Chapter 14: Way Ahead – Action Plan Forms

It was already dark when Travis checked into a little out of the way gasthaus in a small village not too far from the border crossing. It was early evening of the next day and he was exhausted. He made a quick call to Sheila to check in, took a shower and then went to the dining room to enjoy a schnitzel before getting a good night of sleep. He was out as his head touched the pillow.

Meanwhile over that same time frame, Svetlana had given the psychologist a veritable treasure trove of information. It had become convincingly clear that her allegiance to the party in Russia, and to her position in the intelligence services, was directly linked to her efforts to make her own life better. Her comments came across as credible to Janet's interrogator, who had heard similar stories in the past. In fact in recent years it had become a familiar story as more and more members of the Russian system had defected to the West when the opportunities arose.   Svetlana just appeared to have become disillusioned at an earlier age than most.

Of course, even so, it would be for Sheila and for Bob Wallis and the Intel people to confirm she was what she seemed to be. In this business, the worst of all worlds would be to facilitate the entry of a "sleeper" agent into the US structure. But Janet had a lot of experience and this just seemed good at a gut level; and she was developing a good feeling about Svetlana's future value to Tango Section, with proper grooming by Sheila.

Svetlana's little interview had begun this afternoon at about five o'clock as she returned home from a day's work. And it was now about seven thirty in the evening so the toll was starting to show. "Svetlana." Janet started, "You are about to have a very long night and you will have to call in sick in the morning as you recover." Janet had just made a decision, one of her signature "instinct calls," and she was about to share it with this young Russian agent.

"Whatever you are going to do to me, I really would like to eat something first." Svetlana said in reply, "It has been a long day and I need some food, especially if, as you say, it will be a long night." She rubbed her wrists where they had been bound earlier. Janet and the interrogator could see the bruising start to appear on both of her wrists.

Janet stood but motioned for her to stand as well, "That is a reasonable request. But, just grab a little something. I am going to make a call and you are going to have some more visitors this evening. They will verify the things you have told me so far and perhaps they will ask you some more questions." Janet was talking as she moved to the small refrigerator in the efficiency kitchen to retrieve a container of yogurt and a banana from a fruit bowl on the table. As she got to the last statement she could see the tell tale signs of fear starting to show again on Svetlana's face. Her face showed several quick emotions that ranged from concern to fear, as the words sank in.

"Do not worry." Janet held out her hands with palms down in a sort of universal gesture intended to calm the situation. She spoke into the telephone a moment and then put it away as she said, "These people who are coming are very professional and they are not coming to torture you or to hurt you. They will likely use a lie detector and perhaps some drugs. It will be a long night and you will be tired in the morning and likely not able to go to your work. That is why I said what I did, and besides it seems you bruise easily so it would not do to show up at the office with bruises on your wrists and ankles."

"He," Svetlana said indicating the man with the gun, "he is not going to kill me?" Svetlana asked, the worry showing in her words.

"No, if these people who are coming can verify what you have told me then you will be safe. And you will be able to call your boss and explain you have a little cold and a fever. In fact they will also give you a note and a prescription from a doctor that you can show to your boss when you return to work in a day or so." Janet could see Svetlana start to relax and she was even taking small bites of the yogurt she had spooned into a small bowl. She also noted that the banana was already gone and she added, "Oh, and they will bring food too."

That actually got a small smile from her and Svetlana asked, "May I go to the bathroom again before they arrive?"

"Yes, but until I know I can trust you it will be the same as last time. Please understand that we are not some sort of deviants but, I am not going to let you out of my sight quite yet." Janet saw her nod understanding and resignation.

The Next Morning

The day dawned as Janet snoozed half reclining on a small sofa in Svetlana's apartment. The med-techs were packing up their kits and the lie detector tech was doing the same. Svetlana was lying on her bed sleeping off the effects of some of the drugs that had been used on her the previous evening and at various times throughout the night. Finally, someone touched Janet's shoulder and offered her another cup of coffee. She accepted the offered cup gratefully as she sat up, alternately scratching her scalp and running her fingers through her hair and rubbing the sleep out of her eyes.

The lead tech, the one who had handed her the coffee, pulled over a chair and sat across the little space from Janet. He was about to speak when she held up a finger, set down the coffee cup, and excused herself to the bathroom. A moment later the two started the debriefing as Janet sat back down.

Janet was very pleased with the results of the evening's events and she told the team leader as much. Svetlana, the experts all agreed, was what she appeared to be. She was a young, pretty, smart, and disgruntled soviet of the modern generation. And in this case she was ready to be recruited and assigned a handler. The portrait that emerged was one of an orphan, abandoned at birth who had come through a brutal system. Her trials included including being extorted for sex as a young teen by the headmaster of the institution. Then they got down to the details that Sheila and the field team needed now.

"Janet," the lead interrogator said, "Svetlana's boss, is a man named Alfred. By the way, she really does not like or trust him. But more to the point, he has been heard referring to a woman he calls Sonja." The young man saw Janet sit up a little straighter and register a look of recognition at the name. It was as if a cloud moved across her face. He interpreted the look as one of concern as he finished his synopsis, "She figures in this whole operation in some key way or some pivotal role." Then he ran down a quick synopsis of the interrogation results; there was a lot.

"Hold right there please!" Janet ordered holding up a hand to shush him as she reached for the cell phone.

"This is Sheila." Makinley's standard greeting came from the yellow phone on her desk.

"Hi, this is Janet. Is Bob there too?" Janet said into the cell.

"Yes he is hold one." There was a sound like a chair being pulled across the floor then, "Yes we are all here now."

"We have the link to Sonja."

But Janet got no further over the cell phone as she was interrupted. "Did you say Sonja?" Bob interrupted and everyone in the room was instantly alert and focused.

"Yes," Janet answered, "Svetlana believes that this Sonja person is some kind of a lead operator for Alfred. And Svetlana has heard comments that might refer to explosives and a sniper team. Apparently Alfred has to approve the expenditures; and Svetlana has had to do some of the clerical work on more than one occasion. Recently that included typing and filing and other routine tasks. And that is how this came to her attention in the first place."

Sheila interjected, "I am going to ask you to repeat all of that and add any details you might be omitting."

Janet put the cell phone on the little table and waved for the lead tech to repeat everything he had told her earlier. "This is the lead tech on the project." Then to him she said simply, "Go ahead. Tell them everything you told me." Then Janet took a long pull on the coffee and set the cup down on the table beside the phone.

The fellow repeated the last comments and added some details from the questioning and answers by consulting his notes.

"Thank you." Sheila said, "That is extremely helpful. Did she mention anyone else, perhaps from Turkey or Iran?"

"I don't now precisely," the man said and added, "but I believe the man Farouq may fit into that category? She spoke about a man named Farouq who has some sort of family tie-in to this Frankfurt Office." Janet indicated he should continue with this line of discussion, so the man added, "Well, apparently Alfred's predecessor, a man named Sergei, had a son in the Russian Intelligence service and he was 'best friends' at the technical school with this fellow Farouq. Something happened to the son but the father, Sergei, remained close with the young Iranian named Farouq." Then noting the silence on the line the lead tech asked, "Sheila, are you all right? I mean it has been a long night and perhaps we should go over this another time?"

"No, I am fine. Please continue with your findings. And I am going to ask you to get a detailed version of this whole discussion to me as soon as you can. The whole team, including Tango Alpha, will want to hear all of this!" Sheila said recovering her composure, "Please continue and don't leave out any little detail."

The fellow took a moment to review his notes and then started again, "Well, our subject, Svetlana, thinks that Alfred had something to do with his predecessor's removal and perhaps his death as well. She said she did not know if Alfred had engineered Sergei's death but she did say she would 'not be surprised' if he had. In any event Alfred maintains routine contact with Farouq's family in Frankfurt. And Farouq visits Germany from time to time as part of diplomatic visits from Iran to western events."

The young man shifted his weight on the hard chair before he continued, "And that is where this woman named Sonja, who Svetlana has never seen, comes in. She was pretty fuzzy on the exact nature of this relationship but she is convinced that it is all linked somehow. She also believes that Alfred is like an architect and a 'go-between' with his superiors in Moscow; but Sonja is the field operations head who directs the action. Then things got a little jumbled when she tried to sort out where Vladimir, from Dresden, fits into all of this. I just don't know how much of this is speculation, how much is office gossip and how much of it is fact. But, I can tell you with some certainty that Svetlana believes it is all fact."

Chapter 15: Next Steps

Travis awoke glad that he was alone because he was angry. He was angry and he felt strong emotions that he had locked away many, many years ago. It had been a rough night in the little gasthaus as he tried to stay asleep. He kept falling asleep quickly, from exhaustion, but jerking awake with after a short while, with feelings of danger or even fear that Julie was not safe. Then somewhere in the wee hours he managed to stuff it all into a little mental compartment and lock it away at least until this was over. Then he promised himself he could re-open the compartment again, hopefully with Julie near his side, and take a serious look at his emotional self.

A short time later, over morning coffee in the dining area, Travis was almost stoic as he took in his surroundings. His calm exterior masked the mental gymnastics going on inside his head. At one level his gut told him he was making progress and that he would find the guilty bastards and he would kill them. At another level he felt hate and anger competing with regret and the fact that Julie had been drug into his world and she had been hurt. She had been hurt for the sole reason that she had gotten too close to him. And Maria was likely at risk because she ran a business for him.

He was sifting all of this into mental piles of stuff and prioritizing it all for action when the cell phone buzzed. "Yes!" Travis said briskly into the little device.

"This is Hans. Meet me for lunch at one o'clock at my shooting club."

Then the phone went dead. Suddenly Travis had a new issue on which to focus this morning. This had to be something hot for Hans to break silence and risk a meeting. Travis knew the shooting club well and he knew it was a safe, and it was a remote location for members and guests only.

Only Germans could combine shooting and beer, and make a club out of it all. Specifically it was a club that specialized in this combination of activities. Actually, Travis had visited many of these little regional clubs and they all seemed to follow a pattern. After all, the German people were noted for being organized, structured and followers of rules. There was shooting and there was drinking but not at the same time; and all the weapons and ammo were secured away before the first beer was served.

Travis did a little mental math computing the distance and the time it would take to make he trip. It was doable, but just barely; thanks to the German highway system and its high-speed autobahns! He quickly finished his breakfast, paid his bill and thanked the desk clerk for a good night's rest as he left.

Hans' Shooting Club

Most of the members were avid huntsmen and there was a rifle range for them to site in their serious hunting rifles with access to the Jaegermeisters who ran the forest hunts. These were the hunting masters who literally told the hunter which beasts they could shoot. Having the Hunting Masters, or Jaegermeisters, select and approve which to kill was in order to ensure they all culled the weakest from the herd. In this way generations of Jaegermeisters had helped ensure they could maintain the herd integrity and health. They were also the people who ensured the meat was butchered by proper standards and prepared for human consumption.

This particular club, to which Hans belonged, was a larger and better funded one that most Travis had been previously invited to visit. They had substantial land holdings and a large clubhouse on what looked like a private estate. Travis was impressed with the drive through the small forest that obscured the entrance to the place.

But shooting is shooting and the daily fun of the club was the small caliber rifles and target pistols. And of course the competitions between, and among the members and guests were at the indoor ranges of the club building. During these times only coffee, tea and soft drinks were served along with light snacks. But, as soon as the last weapon was locked away and secure, then the bar was open! Some days the pistols never even came out of their secure cases; but the bar did always open!

It was approaching noon as Travis came to the front door and rang the bell. The club steward opened and admitted Travis to a private room where Hans

Feldman was sitting with another man. The man was a stranger and also vaguely familiar. And as Travis searched his memories Hans stood and came to greet him.

"Travis, so good to see you. I know my call was unusual and I think you will understand very soon." Turning to lead Travis the short distance from the room's doorway to the table, Hans indicated the man who was now standing and said, "This man is Ervin and I think you may already know him."

The man called Ervin extended his hand to shake in the western fashion and Travis noticed that two of the fingers were missing their lower joints. Nevertheless the grip was firm and friendly as Ervin said, "Mr. Travis, it is good to see you again. I trust that you and the lady made it successfully from Iran."

Travis felt like he had been hit by a jolt of lightening. This man, Ervin, was the taxi driver who had driven Naja Jade, a deep cover operative, and him across Iran's empty spaces to the coast. He was the unplanned incidental factor that had made it possible for them to sail across the Arabian Gulf in their escape from Iran several years ago. Now Travis grasped the man's hand with both of his hands and said simply, "I pray that you have been blessed for your help on that night."

"That story is what we are here to discuss." Hans said. "And for me, this meeting never happened and I was never here. Do we all understand each other?"

Both Travis and Ervin nodded agreement and understanding, although Travis knew that Hans' words had been spoken for the benefit of the Iranian ex-pat. For Travis and Hans this was just a repeat of the status quo. Travis asked Hans, "Can you stay or must you leave now? And should Ervin and I leave as well?"

"No." Hans said, "In fact it might draw more attention. I have ordered some light food for us to enjoy and then we will part company. I trust you will give Ervin a ride to wherever he needs to go?"

"Of course I will." Travis said, and then added with a smile, "He once did the same for me." Then conversation stopped while the waiter brought the food and drinks.

As the waiter withdrew and closed the door, Hans said, "I was working on immigration duty when Ervin just happened to come for asylum a few years ago. He was with his wife and daughter. But the badly bandaged hand caught my attention and we got him to proper medical treatment. Then I dug a little deeper into his story because I had seen such injuries before. And they were almost always either from torture of some sort or from farm equipment, and he did not look like a farmer." That last was delivered with a smile from Hans and a reciprocal smile from Ervin and then from Travis.

Here Ervin interjected, "Travis, You never met my wife Ashti or my daughter Baharak. They are two women as beautiful as their names. Ashti means 'peace' and she always seeks peace in her life and has brought that to my life as well. Our daughter's name means 'little spring' and she has brought all the goodness into our life, especially here in Germany where we have been well received." He paused just a moment and added, "And that is due in part to the fateful meeting with you in the desert village where we lived before."

Hans saw the quizzical look on Travis' face as Ervin started his story. "Travis, it will all be clear in just a moment, let me explain further. I was on duty processing this little family and trying to get a medic over to look at Ervin's infected hand as I said when he told me the most incredible tale."

Travis ate a little and listened in silence as Hans told the story with only occasional interruptions by Ervin. "In Iran, this man Ervin had been the owner and operator of the only taxi in his village on the edge of the desert. At least that had been his life before the Syrian trader had come to him one night with a request."

Ervin took over the narrative, "This Syrian trader asked me to take him and his woman to the shore of Iran in the middle of the night. It had seemed a little unusual because there was nothing in that part of the coast but he was willing to pay my price. In fact that was what first piqued my curiosity because he was so bad at negotiating." Travis sat up a little straighter looking at Ervin, who continued without missing a beat, "I mean Syrian traders are notoriously tight with money and will negotiate anything any time. So I was thinking maybe this man is not a real Syrian. But it was a slow night so I did take them into the desert almost to the coast and I stayed and watched from a distance."

"You stayed and watched?" Travis asked, mentally making notes on his need to brush up his own tradecraft.

"Yes," Ervin said, "If he was not a real Syrian trader then maybe she was not his wife either. So, I dropped the two people near the shore and withdrew a safe distance to watch a while for what might happen next. But the first thing I saw was the man and woman arguing so I figured 'yes' they really are married and I started to leave." That got a chuckle from Travis and Hans as they all picked at their food.

Ervin took a bite or two and continued his account, "Anyway, the man who had been arguing took off his clothes and dove into the water several times. You know what I thought? The way he was diving I thought maybe he was a pearl diver or something. But he stayed underwater a little longer than was normal and then a strange boat had popped up to the surface of the water. A short time after that with some more arguing, the man and the woman just sailed away across the gulf between Iran and Saudi Arabia."

"Later I told the story of that night to my wife and my daughter." Ervin paused just a second and added, "Of course I left out the part about the woman taking off her clothes and changing into swimming clothes. My wife did not need to know that the woman was very physically beautiful, even in the desert night."

Travis dropped all pretenses and agreed, "Yes, Ervin, she is a very beautiful woman and she is safely now where she belongs to be."

Ervin picked up the narrative again, "As I said, I told the story to my wife and daughter, much to their amusement and amazement, the next morning and then we forgot about the whole thing." There was a change that came across his face and Hans reached out a hand to touch the man's forearm almost as if to give him strength. Ervin nodded to Hans and then cleared his throat and started again.

"And by the next day we had almost forgotten about it all until the men from Farouq came to take me and my wife and daughter for questioning. The questioning did not go well and the man called Farouq was brutal in a merciless way." Ervin raised his hand and wiggled the stubs where his fingers had once been, "Farouq cut away parts of my fingers one joint at a time in the process of asking questions and not getting the answers he wanted."

"You must have been a very brave and stubborn man for Farouq to do these things." Travis said and then added, "And I fear I am in your debt for what you have endured."

"Wait, there is more." Ervin said hurrying to continue.

Ervin started but Hans inserted himself into the story. "And this is where I must leave you two. I fear the conversation might border on discussion that might sound like a conspiracy. I cannot be part of any such discussion because of my official duties." And Hans stood to leave.

"Hans, I owe you and your people so very much. And now you offer me a way to help with retribution against Farouq." Ervin stood and placed a hand on Hans' shoulder.

But Hans interrupted again more forcefully, "Gentlemen, I did not hear a word of that and I really must not be here. Stay as long as you like in my club. You are a member's guests and you will not be disturbed." And with that, he left without another word but he did wink at his two guests.

There was only a moment of quiet and Ervin resumed his account. "Farouq brought my wife and daughter into the room where he had me tied to a chair cutting away my fingers. They were naked and ashamed and this man held them both by their hair, like some sort of animals. He threatened them and said he would kill each while I watched before he killed me if I lied again."

Ervin hung his head, "So I broke and told him everything I could tell him and he did at least release us all. We started that day to find a way to leave Iran and what it has become under the Republican Guards. When we finally made our way to the German border we met Hans and he listened and believed and has helped us start our new life."

"Mr. Travis, Hans says I can trust you and I believe I may be able to help you. I am not a fool and I know you are a very dangerous man. But you were there to rescue the woman you passed off as your wife. That takes an honorable man to do such a thing for a woman who is not even his family. But I am here today because one day last year I saw Farouq here in Germany."

Ervin took a sip of his after lunch coffee and continued, "I saw him here on the streets of Frankfurt. I have followed him and observed him and he comes routinely to see the Russian at the diplomatic mission here. He has a family here and I have followed him to see them and I know where they are. Therefore I know exactly where he will be at some time in the very near future."

"Ervin," Travis started, "I think that you and I are about to become friends united by a bond of common interests and justice." Internally, Travis was starting to dislike these people, around Alfred, more and more with everything he learned about them.

A little later that evening after he had dropped Ervin near his home, when he was alone, Travis called Sheila and told her about Ervin. It was clear that the team were appreciative for the role that Ervin could, and would play to avenge the mistreatment of his family. This personal reason tied in nicely with what was to come. And Sheila agreed that Ervin could be rewarded when this was laid to bed and that if something went wrong his wife and daughter would be cared for.

Chapter 16: Hard Part - Wait & Watch

It was quite a pleasant day in Frankfurt and the weather was even cooperating for a change. The sun could be seen peeking between the clouds, and around the tall buildings, and it was warm enough to enjoy the sidewalk café they had found. Travis liked that there were enough people on the street, and moving around them, that they were invisible. Then Ervin tensed and leaned forward across the little table towards Travis.

"That is him." Ervin said in a whisper but Trav could hear the tension in his voice even so. "That is Farouq. That is the man who humiliated me and threatened the life of my wife and my daughter. He is the man who cut off the ends of my fingers." Travis put a hand on Ervin's forearm to calm him and to help him regain his composure.

The two men had spent the morning sitting at a table in a local café where Ervin sipped a cup of tea while Travis nursed his mug of coffee. There was nothing remarkable about the two men who looked like office workers on a long work break. They talked about everything from soccer to sports in general and even about the weather.

Their only task for this morning was to wait and watch. Trav had been alerted by Bob Wallis and his friends that Farouq had appeared on a flight manifest arriving in Frankfurt early this morning. He had reasoned that Farouq would eventually appear at Alfred's office; but he had bet that Farouq would surely visit his sister and her family as a first stop.

And again Trav's gut paid off. Travis and Ervin watched the Iranian exit a taxi with an armload of bags and packages. He was just across the street at the front steps of a huge old house that had been converted into apartments at some time in the past. The packages he was carrying were obviously gifts for the children and for his sister.

This was an older, more established neighborhood and a solid middle class location. It was within walking distance of stores and kiosks where fresh produce and vegetables were available. And there was even a butcher shop within a couple of blocks of the café at which they were seated. This would be a very nice place for a Middle Eastern woman with her two children to live a quiet and peaceful life. Trav and Ervin waited patiently sipping their beverages and then settled the bill, leaving a modest tip, and left the café together.

When they had reached the end of the block they stopped at the back of an old Mercedes services van with the utility logo on the side and took a quick look around. Neither man saw anything and when Travis nodded, Ervin reached out and opened one side of the double doors on the back of the van. It was crowded with the three men already in the vehicle. Two men sat on little swing out stools, looking intently at some sort of computer array built into the interior wall of the panel truck. They were obviously monitoring the interior of the apartment where Farouq was even now greeting his sister and her children.

The children on the little screen, in the middle of the equipment, clustered on the inside wall of the van, showed two children running around and screaming with delight. There were four such screens in total with different views of the apartment. The children could be seen running from one screen into the field of vision of the one beside it, or sometimes below, the center screen. The other technician was monitoring the voice level and recording everything. The third fellow, whose name was Emilio, moved to the front of the van pressing his back against the driver's seat to make room for Trav and Ervin. Emilio nodded to the two and asked simply, "Target confirmed?"

"Yes." Travis and Ervin said simultaneously and then Ervin spoke again, "That is definitely the man, Farouq, who is a senior official of the IRGC in my home area of Iran. He is the fellow who cut away my fingers to torture me." Travis noted that Ervin did not mention the demeaning treatment of his wife and daughter to these strangers.

"Have we heard anything from across town?" Travis asked the third man.

"Yes, just as you two were entering the van I got a call that Alfred had left the building. They said he almost ran to his car in the garage and is headed our way now." Emilio said. The he added, "And Svetlana just let us know she is also on the move. She has been sent out to pick up the woman, Sonja, and bring her back to the office for a meeting of some sort very shortly today."

One of the techies interrupted, "Hey Emilio, the target just told his sister that he has to go out to meet a business associate for a very important meeting." Holding up a finger to signal silence he continued to listen then said, "But he will be back in a couple of hours." Pausing just a second but holding up a finger again so they would wait, he added, "The sister says she hates that he must go out already. But if he promises to come back this evening she will cook a piece of lamb and they will celebrate with the children when he returns."

The other techie cut into his report with an input of his own, "Gentlemen, a grey German Ford with diplomatic tags, just pulled up and parked illegally in front of the house. It is just sitting there with the motor running. The driver is wearing a dark suit and he looks nervous."

Travis leaned to look over the man's shoulder almost cheek to cheek with the fellow and said, "Yes that is Alfred from the Cultural Attaché Office. I am guessing he came himself because he is trying to control all the details. He is also trying to keep others out of the loop about his role in this thing." Travis looked over at Emilio, "Do we know exactly what this thing is yet?"

Emilio replied almost immediately, "Yes. Bob Wallis sent word that they are concerned that Sonja's guys may have overdone it in Spain. It appears she and Alfred had quite a disagreement over an open phone line. Travis, I know this is difficult for you after they wounded your friend trying to lure you out." Then as Travis nodded his thanks, Emilio added, "Alfred thinks that Sonja has jeopardized their other planned hits. Apparently, Sonja is acting as some kind of field ops director while Alfred and Farouq call the shots."

Travis cut in, "So who is in charge? Alfred?"

"Yes, sir." Emilio said, "Bob says his guys have concrete proof that Alfred gets approval in general terms from Moscow through Dresden, of all places. It is interesting that they are bypassing Bonn and Berlin. But clearly, somebody in Moscow approves everything."

"Sounds like 'plausible deniability,' to me." Travis said.

"That sounds like a lot of trouble they took to keep their 'fingerprints' off this thing." Emilio said in response. Emilio started to add something else but stopped when he glanced over at Travis and Ervin.

Travis caught the look and asked, "Emilio do we need to step outside a moment?"

"Yes." Emilio said but when he saw the questions in Ervin's eyes he added, "Just some office admin details to discuss with Travis, you guys keep watching and recording."

Safely outside with no one around Travis asked, "What's up?"

"Sheila said to pass along to you as soon as I got a chance that there does not appear to be a leak internally. She and Bob ran polygraphs on everybody and added a few drugs to the questioning in some cases. They theorize that what we thought might be a leak was actually the info flow in former KGB/FSB channels feeding this guy Putin in Dresden and through him to Alfred." Emilio finished but kept scanning the area around them for strangers.

"That does help put my mind at ease." Travis said and added, "Thanks. Shall we go back in?"

As they reentered the van Emilio saw the look that passed between Travis and Ervin. The two men exchanged a look, a glance really, but the look in their eyes gave Emilio pause. Both men had a look as cold as any that Emilio had ever seen. Travis spoke in a deadpan voice, "There will be time to reflect on all of this later. But right now we have work to do before these assholes attack or kill any more of our field operatives."

Then verbally shifting gears so as not to kill any fruitful discussion, Travis added, "So Farouq is the connective tissue to the Middle East through his power position in the IRGC. And, he leverages that same power to exploit the PJAK and their Kurdish links into Turkey and Iraq and throughout the region.

And of course Farouq has feelers into the refugee community here and elsewhere in Europe."

"And," Emilio added, "Alfred gives deniability to the diplomatic mission here in Germany if something goes sideways because he has 'officially' left Bonn and Berlin out of the loop. He has been dealing directly only with this guy in Dresden, who by the way hasn't been there very long and seems to have inserted himself, according to Bob and his people. This is a perfect set up for deniability and could be made to look like They have an operative gone rogue." Then Emilio added, "So what about Sonja?"

Trav spoke up. "About five years ago on a previous mission to bring someone in from the cold, in Iran, Sonja tried to take me out but the attempt did not go well for her. She wound up in our custody, along with two of her thugs, so this is likely personal as well as professional for her. That might explain why she went to such an extreme measure trying to lure me out into the open." What Travis did not say and did not need to say, at least to this group, was that he intended to make sure she was never a threat again.

Across Town

Ironically as the group, packed into the van, was having this conversation, Svetlana was picking Sonja up for transport to the Office of the Cultural attaché. The two women were not friends and in fact were barely acquainted. This was the first time Svetlana had time and the opportunity to study Sonja as they drove along. She was struck by the fact that there could be no more than ten years difference between the two of them. And yet Sonja looked to be at least twenty years older than Svetlana. Her face had the sunken eye, hollow look of a drug addict, and she was emaciated as though she had recently lost a lot of weight too quickly.

What Svetlana did not know was that Sonja was making her own assessment of her. Sonja saw what she referred to as the "new generation of Communists" when she was talking among her friends. Her friends, on the other hand she described as "serious Communists" and they were quite different from this new generation who most often seemed to be "out for themselves."

For them, Sonja had decided, everything was about how these new Communists could improve their personal situation. Admittedly there had always been that tendency among the overseas cadre of Soviets, but they were all agreed on the need to advance the cause of world communism. That bond of agreement seemed to have evaporated in this emerging contemporary atmosphere. This young woman beside her, driving the car, was wearing a tailored suit and expensive shoes and smelled of an expensive perfume. In other words, Svetlana typified everything that Sonja might have once admired but had now come to hate.

Chapter 17: Meeting; Then Back To Home

Sitting in the car at the curb, Alfred did not have long to wait. Farouq came down stairs just a couple of minutes after Alfred arrived in front of the sister's home. At that point Travis turned to Ervin and said, "Now we sleep."

"What?" Ervin asked incredulously.

Before Trav could say anything Emilio spoke up, "Trust Travis. He is right. In an operation like this you sleep when you can because you never know when the next opportunity for sleep will come."

"Ervin, I know that you and I both are feeling pretty tense right now," Travis said, "but we can do nothing here that these tech experts can not do better. When we wake, we will have the feedback of their meeting from Svetlana. This will come as soon as she can get away from the meeting at Alfred's office. And the next action will not come until that meeting is concluded."

Travis could see that Ervin was not convinced, as he added, "There is information we need about this next action of theirs. They are making plans to kill my friends and I need that information before we deal with them individually. But I promise you we will deal with them. It just will be at a time and a place of our choosing and we will get them all."

And, for his part, Emilio was a still little uncomfortable that this might go sideways if Ervin went on his own as he spoke, "We have a safe house just a short distance from here where you two can get a little rest." Emilio added, "And I will call as soon as anything changes. Now go and rest, while you can."

Travis took Ervin's arm and steered him out of the van. He and Ervin walked together about two blocks and Travis turned to lead the way down a short, nondescript alley. A third of the way into the alley he turned sharply and stepped around a trash dumpster to enter a half obscured doorway. The two men went inside and were met by a very fit looking young man with a pistol in his hand.

Travis waited calmly while the fellow, clearly recognizing Travis, put his pistol away and opened the door behind himself. Travis and Ervin squeezed past and were in a kind of reception area where a "clerk," who also had a pistol visible and within his reach, looked up from his desk. "Sleep and a shower, I assume." the fellow said and handed Travis and Ervin a fresh towel, a pillow, and a folded set of clean underwear. Then he asked, "Do you need a pill?"

Travis answered for the two of them, "No, we have to be fresh when we leave so just some quiet." Then taking the folded pile of things he added, "Thank you."

Turning to Ervin he said, "I would suggest a quick shower first because you will rest better and then sleep or rest as you can. There will not be time to shower when the call comes. When it does come, we will leave immediately." Ervin just nodded in disbelief at the whole surreal situation.

Time To Move

The door opened to the small room where Ervin slept, and as light streamed in, Travis filled the doorway, "Time to go, Ervin."

Ervin was up surprisingly fast, "You were right. The shower helped," he said, "But I still had trouble getting to sleep. Where are we going now?"

"We are walking back to the van. The meeting just ended and it appears that Alfred will be joining Farouq for the evening meal at the sister's home. And we will be watching and listening to everything." Travis answered the man as they started moving and then added, "They will likely have a proper feast but we will be drinking bad coffee and eating cold sandwiches."

With that Ervin actually smiled. The two men made the trip in short order and, seeing no one around, were in the back of the van in a matter of minutes. Emilio was still there but the techies from earlier had been replaced by a woman and another man. As they squeezed in, Emilio offered them a couple of disposable cups and a thermos of coffee.

Travis and Ervin accepted the coffee smiling their thanks as Emilio started talking, "Svetlana is driving Sonja back to her residence and then she will be meeting with our people for a thorough debrief.

While you slept she did manage to pass to one of our contacts a note when the group broke for lunch. I have that here if you would like to see it." He held out a small piece of paper to Travis.

Travis took it and read, the letter "A" with a circle around it the letter "F" with a circle around it and the letter "S" with a circle around it as well. The text said, "A = #1, F = #2, S = having bad day. A and F pissed at S for not following plan. S says will follow future. A and F plan more action very soon. S making notes."

Travis cleared his throat and asked Emilio, "Are we set for a detailed debrief with Svetlana this evening?"

"Yes, Travis, we are, and the details of that will be fed to us here in real time." Emilio answered, "You will know everything as fast as we do." Travis glanced over at Ervin who was clearly amazed at the organization of this whole operation, then looked back to Emilio. "OK, gentlemen. It is show time." Emilio said tapping one of the monitors, "It looks as though Alfred and Farouq have arrived."

Family Dinner

From the monitors the techies watched as Farouq entered the house first and greeted his sister and the kids. Then he presented Alfred who offered his hand to Samira, Farouq's sister. But Samira pushed his hand aside and stepped forward to hug him and said, "Alfred, you are my uncle in our adopted country. You have always treated my family so well. I thank you and say that you are always welcome here as family, just as Sergei was before you."

Farouq smiled at Alfred and Alfred relaxed, then acting as if he had just remembered the bag of presents the children had been eyeing. Alfred made a show of looking down at his side and at the bag he held, as he feigned surprise. As they became more and more excited, Alfred extracted presents for the children.

With each small package they hugged his legs then, afterward they ran off to play with their new toys. Alfred pulled out one last gift that was not wrapped and he saw the smile on Samira's face immediately. Alfred handed the American made coffee to the lady of the house. "It is a small thing, I know but it is all for you, I doubt the children will want to share it."

Again Samira smiled, "Uncle Alfred, you know me so well. I do love the American coffee and I thank you for bringing me my favorite treat." Then she turned to Farouq and said, "Why don't you men go in and have a seat at the table. I will be in shortly with something to eat." Then she came immediately behind them with a tray of soft drinks and water with glasses and some ice in a dish. She set the tray between them on the table and excused herself.

A short time later, when they ate the evening meal, she served the two men. Then tactfully, she excused herself again and withdrew to eat her own meal in the kitchen so they were able to talk freely. "Farouq, you have honored me this day with your presence and your grasp of the situation. And now this evening, you have opened your family's home to me. I am forever in your debt." Alfred said by way of transitioning the conversation to more serious matters.

"Alfred, you are always welcome and I cannot thank you enough for continuing to care for my sister and the children after Sergei passed away." Farouq said softly.

"Yes," Alfred started to repeat the lie and the false sense of loss that he had learned to project, "That was a very sad event indeed. And I knew that the two of you had been close after the American murdered Sergei's only son. It seemed the least I could do." Alfred feigned humility.

"At the risk of inserting work back into a really pleasant evening," Farouq started, adding, "do you think Sonja understood the message?"

"Oh, my friend, she definitely got the message." Alfred said a little too quickly.

Farouq replied with a little more emphasis, "Oh, I believe she got the message, but did she understand it? Do you think she understands that her life is in peril if she goes her own way again? I would hate for her to ruin all the careful and painstaking work you have orchestrated so that we may make the next move in the game. The next move will remove three at once form the face of the earth."

Back in the van Emilio whispered, "Go ahead, you bastard, tell us more. Just tell us where and when, you son of a bitch."

But in the house, the conversation changed abruptly as Samira could be heard herding the children into the room where the men were talking. "The children wanted to thank you again for the gifts and they want to say good night before I put them to bed." She said smiling and then lowered her voice to add, "And I will make a cup of your gift to me and come back to join you two as soon as I can get them into their beds."

"That would be wonderful." Alfred said adding, "Don't you agree Farouq?"

"Yes, yes, of course. After all, it is your house my honored sister. We will always do as you want." Farouq said with real affection in his voice for his sister.

Meanwhile the men outside, who were packed into the van parked on the street near the house, watched and listened intently. But Ervin had had all that he could stand and finally spoke out, "See how he pretends to live a normal life? This is the animal that chained me to a chair and removed my finger joints," Ervin held up his disfigured hand as he continued, "one knuckle at a time with a pair of cutting pliers."

Travis could tell that Ervin was becoming emotional because he did not stop the story this time. He added, "Then while still helpless and chained to the chair, he paraded my wife and daughter naked in front of me. I was helpless and humiliated as his thugs held them by a handful of hair, one in each hand, and threatened them with torture. He said he would kill my daughter in front of me and my wife. Then he said he would kill my wife in front of me, before he killed me."

"Ervin," Travis interrupted, "are you alright?"

"No, I am not!" Ervin replied, "I want to run into his house and kill him now. No, that is not true. I want to do to him what he said he would do to me, kill his family in front of him." Then, just as Travis thought he might have to remove the man from the van, Ervin seemed to calm and said quietly, "But that would not be just! The sister and her children, they have done nothing to me." Ervin took a deep breath and added, "Just leave me alone with him when this is over."

The technical men in the van looked at each other and Emilio looked at Travis. Travis placed a hand on Ervin's shoulder but did not say anything. The moment passed and they all returned to their duties.

Chapter 18: Sembach Air Base

A call came to the van and an hour and a half later, Travis was waiting in a lounge of sorts at Sembach Air Base in Germany because it was the closest that worked for his needs. Ervin had been told to stay with Emilio for further instructions, or at least until Travis returned. And now, Travis was awaiting the arrival of a small executive jet that would take him to Madrid for an emergency meeting with Sheila and Bob at Torrejon Air Base. He barely had time to sit when a young Sergeant entered and said, "Mr. Lemon, please follow me, your aircraft is here."

The flight was relatively short and bypassed all the normal immigration and customs requirements by using the DV lounges for diplomatic travel. To save time, operational time, they eliminated the car ride for Travis to the Us Embassy Compound where Tango Section was housed. He found them waiting in a secure room at Operations Center on Torrejon Air Base. Sheila and Bob were there with Tango Alpha at the head of the table.

"Travis, please come in and sit down." The "old man" said. He was as gracious as always and indicated a chair beside him at the table.

Travis thanked him and acknowledged the others at the table before he spoke. "Sir," Travis said addressing the Head of Tango Section, "I know we have a part of the picture but we do not have the whole thing. I assume that is why you called me in from the field."

"Astute, as always, Tango 5." The Agency Head said, "But there is more and I felt we should all discuss face-to-face." Then turning to Sheila he added, "Would you begin please, Sheila." It was not a question.

Sheila did not hesitate to lay out the outline they had come up with in the HQ. "We believe there is a sanction from Russia with plausible deniability that basically allows Alfred to settle old scores for himself and for his predecessor."

Travis moved to speak but Sheila raised a finger and said, "I know it is not perfect but it is a working framework, so please let me get through this thing and we can refine as needed." Travis sat back and waited. He knew Sheila well and he knew her work, and he knew that after Istanbul, she had some skin in the game as well. He had thought often about being side by side with her near the Hagia Sophia. The bomb that went off in the assassination attempt that could have taken them both out for good.

"As I was saying." she began again enumerating the assumptions, "One, we think there is a loose sanction from Moscow with over watch by this guy Putin in Dresden. That allows deniability and that gives Alfred free reign here. Two, we think Alfred seems to be calling the shots with assistance from Farouq in a kind of symbiotic 'senior partner, junior partner' relationship. Three, we think that Sonja was set up to have a kind of chief of field ops role but she may have gone rogue. And she has 'hands on' control of the shooters and bomb makers in Europe."

Sheila paused just a moment to let that all sink in and then added, "Her role is much like that played by Farouq in the Middle East but without the 'vote' or influence with Alfred. And finally four, we should not rule out the implication that this new player in the game, Vladimir Putin, is the current FSI Chief in Dresden. Of course that means he was KGB previously. Sergei was also KGB previously so there is the chance they knew each other in 'the good old days.' So the over watch of Alfred may have greater implications than we realize. " She paused and indicated that Travis should comment.

"Actually, that sounds about right but I need to question one of the opening assumptions." Travis said turning to Bob Wallis, who for once did not have the intel guys all aligned half way down one side of the table, "Bob, didn't you guys have something previously that indicated this guy, Alfred, was likely involved if not responsible for the death of his boss, Sergei?"

Bob Wallis leaned forward uncomfortable with the limelight. "Yes, that appears likely." He said but offered nothing further.

"So," Travis continued, "If he killed his old boss why would he now be following up on the guy's personal hit list, that by the way, seems to start with me."

Before Bob could answer, Sheila spoke up, "I believe I can answer that one." She said smoothly, "As I recall Alfred set up his boss and made sure that his sponsor back in Moscow knew what Sergei was doing that was, to paraphrase, 'off the rails' and a potential embarrassment to Moscow. Moscow concurred and cut their losses, so to speak, by recalling Sergei, ordering him home, and putting Alfred in his position. The actual 'auto accident' back in Russia that killed Sergei was just one of their 'unavoidable things that happen,' as they say."

Travis nodded once and Sheila pressed ahead to finish her point, "And more to the point, yes, Sergei did want you dead after that incident where you killed his son in El Salvador a few years ago." That got Trav's attention she could tell from his reaction and she continued, "Travis, we know now that Farouq and Sergei's son, Nikolai, were classmates at the technical school that Russia runs to provide training for their field operatives."

Travis reached for the coffee pot in front of him, and poured a cup as Sheila spoke. "Damn." He exclaimed, "This thing just never ends, does it?"

"Oh," Sheila said, "they have long memories and it gets better. The woman, Sonja, remember the stewardess from a few years ago?"

"Yes, she drugged my drink and almost killed me." Travis answered.

"Well, you wouldn't recognize her now, hooked on drugs, aging quickly and a little unhinged mentally. Well, she was apparently romantically involved with Nikolai."

Travis paused with cup in mid-air, "Shit! Are you serious?"

"Yes, very serious." Sheila replied, "That is a part of why we asked you to come down for a face-to-face, so you know what we have put together about what you are facing, but wait it gets better." Sheila took a sip of her own coffee, then added, "Remember the two thugs that you overpowered in Germany after Sonja drugged you? Well, the one you stabbed, whose name is Heinrich, we believe is the shooter who shot and tried to kill Julie."

"And," Sheila continued on a roll, "the one whose nose you bloodied was named Hansel. He is the guy we found dead when we located the shooter's hideout in the hills around Alicante. He was part of the team so we speculate he was the spotter. And that team bombed your home and shot Julie."

They worked for Sonja then, and they work for Sonja now. The only twist that makes sense is that Heinrich killed Hansel, and that was likely on the orders of Sonja. All of this points to Sonja becoming unhinged; well even more murderous than the other two Alfred and Farouq.

"Sheila, why are they still alive? When I left them for you and the cleanup team that night in the hotel I assumed you would get the information you could and then terminate them."

The room had become suddenly tense and there was an awkward silence finally broken when the "Old Man" spoke. "Let's take a little bathroom break and reconvene in fifteen minutes," and turning to Travis he added, "Tango 5, would you stay behind just a moment please?" The two of them walked off into a corner of the room as everyone else left to find the restrooms.

As soon as the door was closed behind the last one leaving, Tango Alpha turned to face Travis, "Are you all right, young man?" he said and placed a hand on Trav's arm as a father might.

Travis looked deeply into the old man's eyes and answered honestly, "No, sir, I am not all right. But I am forcing it all into a cubbyhole, stuffed in along with my emotions, and I will lock it down shortly, at least until we get this thing resolved."

"I am taking you at your word, because I trust your professionalism; but also because we have no choice. Tango #3 Johnson is dead and so is Tango #6 Kinderson; and that lies squarely at my feet." Travis just looked at his Agency Head dumbfounded as the old man continued, "You and Sheila barely escaped in Istanbul. Your beloved Julie was shot, and Sheila will tell us in a minute how we have indications that they plan a triple killing of our operatives in a matter of days."

The Old Man took a deep breath and continued, "Those three are aware they are part of the bait and with Tango #1 Vega still in recovery, and unable to walk well, my boy, you are it. I need you to stop this and end it once and for all." The two of them just looked at each other a moment in a sort of communication without words and then finally Travis just nodded his head once and they broke the gaze.

"Now," the older man said, "one more thing. It was my decision not to terminate those three people who now cause us such distress. I made that call despite their role in trying to stop your mission to rescue my daughter from deep cover in Iran. So blame me, heaven knows I do blame myself. And you are the first to know that once this mess is cleared up I plan to retire and leave the service for good. This whole thing makes me question my own judgment."

Travis was dumbfounded and just looked at Tango Alpha, who continued to speak, "Sheila will take over temporarily to rebuild while the big kids in DC select a new head of the agency. I tell you this because she will need you to get her through the tough times ahead. You take care of the field and keep it alive and going and she will fight the battle with the bureaucrats. Then you and Julie should think about a quiet life for a while someplace away from everyone."

Then shifting the conversation again he said simply, "Now, why don't you and I use the facilities through that door over there and freshen ourselves up. The others will be back in a moment and waiting for you and me." Travis went through the door indicated and his senior followed him into the men's room.

When Travis and Tango Alpha came back into the room from the restroom he found Elizabeth Barclay waiting. She whispered something to the old man and then he turned away and headed to a waiting car that Travis saw had police escort.

"Travis, Sheila, Bob" Elizabeth said, "I am sorry I had to pull him away but I can tell you he gave me specific instructions to pass along. He said I should tell you all his thoughts and prayers are with you all. And Travis he said he was sincerely sorry for the attack on the special person in your life. He also said that he sincerely wishes you could be there for her as she recovers and comes to terms with what it is you do." Then she straightened her back and wiped a single tear from her eye. "And this part is from me, please go and kill these bastards!" Then to the others, "Before I leave to follow him, is there anything any of you need before we send Travis back to the Lear Jet outside?"

Meeting And Time For Talk Ends

The look in Trav's eyes was a cold as any she had ever seen as he said simply, "I will be OK. And," pausing just a second, "thank you all for everything. But right now I guess I better get back to work." He looked towards the door of the room as Sheila started to speak but Travis cut her off with a comment, "Sorry, Sheila, but let me say that this little group of psychopaths has a successful op running. That op is gutting our organizational capabilities, and I need everything you have to be able to stop it." Then looking to her, "Is that about right?"

"We all need to sit for about ten more minutes." Sheila said with authority in her voice and Travis and Bob sat as Barclay left the room.

Travis listened and participated as appropriate as the team made him as ready as they possibly could. He was not concerned for the three operatives who were to be the bait. He knew them all personally and they were solid. Tango #2, a guy named Ellerbe, had served time in the Army when Travis had been in the USAF and they had been in many of the same places but had not known each other back then.

Tango #4, a lady named Smithfield, was a tennis pro and had reflexes and physical skills that were the envy of all. She always travelled with her husband who was also her trainer and himself a former Navy Seal. The joke was that the agency got a two for one deal with them. And Tango #7 was a guy named Jones and he was maybe the strongest man Trav had ever met, but he was not a body builder. He looked more like a dockworker or a deliveryman for a furniture company. He was a large black man who was always very polite and absolutely invisible when hiding in plain sight. He had been a college instructor on track for a full professorship when he had made the career change to covert ops.

As the time approached for Trav to head back to his aircraft he asked, "Is that about it?"

"It is." Sheila replied simply, "Let's do this! Shall we?" But that last was not a question and everyone at the table and in the room knew it.

Travis said some quick thanks and goodbyes, and headed back outside where the engines were already running on his flight back to the airbase in Germany.

Chapter 19: Interrogation

By the time Travis got back to Germany the next steps were already underway. He joined the team conducting the interrogations just as they were getting underway. First on his agenda was a visit to the room where Alfred was being held after a snatch and grab mission early this morning.

"Why did you try to kill my friend in Spain?" Travis asked as Alfred began to regain consciousness. When there was no response he repeated the question, "I said, why did you try to kill my friend in Spain?"

The mind is a powerful thing and it can be your best friend or your worst enemy. It can reinforce your belief system and affirm your life decisions when you are on solid ground. It can also bring everything into question when you find you are on unfamiliar ground and feel yourself at risk. Travis was counting on the later, in this case, because it appeared that Alfred did not have a lot of field experience.

In his own experience Travis had found that a firm commitment to a set of well thought out objectives was essential. Similarly, a plan in which he had confidence, would take him through a lot of doubt. Alfred did not have this experience and Travis was counting on this lack of experience. And of course for perhaps for the first time in his like Alfred was faced with the reality of "getting his hands dirty" by facing danger himself, up close and personal. This was likely something he did not have the mental discipline to endure.

At least that was what Travis hoped in this case. Travis did not like to use torture because he hated the idea and the practice. But the fact that he abhorred physical torture did not stop him from creating an impression, and a belief, in the mind of the adversary that he might se it. And belief could be a successful tactic, especially if applied against an adversary who himself was part of a system that did in fact practice torture on a regular basis.

Travis leaned into Alfred's face and repeated the words very quietly this time, almost a whisper, "Why did you try to kill my friend in Spain?"

"I do not know what you are talking about." Alfred mumbled. The drugs were taking effect and he was having trouble resisting the bombardment of questions. Travis stood as if to strike him, and saw that Alfred flinched anticipating the blow. But there was no blow, Travis was an action-oriented fellow but the violence he committed was aimed at a purpose. And the drugs were so much more effective; they just needed a little more time to work.

The challenge was not just to do a snatch and grab with Alfred and Farouq. The challenge was to get them to talk in time to round up the hit-teams stalking the three Tango Section Operatives, and to neutralize the threat. And of course the other part of the problem was doing it all so fast that they were not setting off alarm bells in Dresden or for that matter Moscow itself. In other words, he did not want not to give a warning, to whoever was really running this Op, in time for him or her to react, or to make a counter-move.

These thoughts were running rampant through Trav's mind but outwardly he appeared as though all was calm and under control. Travis merely turned to the other man present in the little room with him and Alfred, and said, "Go ahead. Use a little more of your drugs to get him to talk. It seems he is almost ready to tell us what we want to know. I will be back after a while." Travis continued out of the door as the other man filled a syringe and began to inject its contents into Alfred's arm. Alfred looked more terrified at the syringe than he had been at the potential of Travis' blow.

Travis headed to the other room, which was just a few feet away in another soundproof cubicle. In fact, it was just next-door and as he entered he saw that Ervin was holding a pair of pliers. Ervin moved the tool in front of Farouq's face and was saying something in Farsi. It was clear that Farouq was starting to realize the seriousness of his situation as Travis took up a position to the left rear of Ervin.

He and Ervin had talked at length after the outburst in the surveillance van. Travis was confident that Ervin was back under control but he wanted to stay and observe for a few minutes just to be sure.

And, of course, that would also give the drugs time to work on Alfred in the next room.

Ervin understood there were rewards, for him personally and for his family, for helping; but not for losing control and just extracting revenge. Travis had explained patiently and in detail since the first encounter at the hunt club of his GSG9 friend. There would be a financial reward if this was all successful and the best revenge is always living well. Travis was finally satisfied that Ervin understood, that he and his small family would reap the benefits of living well in a free nation.

They would have a chance at a better life than they could have ever imagined in Iran. And his daughter would have a world open to her that would not have been possible before. All he had to do was stick with the plan and help extract the information they needed. Travis had wrapped it all up with the statement that, in this way, the disfigured hand could be a badge of honor in his new life. Travis had told him that in a future time he would boast about the lost fingertips being the price he paid for his family's future.

Ervin had liked that argument but he also wanted to instill a little of the terror he had felt at Farouq's hands. As Ervin had told Travis, it was because he felt his honor demanded it. Travis understood that particular emotion. In fact right now he shared it as he dealt with his own feelings of vulnerability after the attack on Julie. This was barbarism on a new scale and personified in a senseless series of attacks orchestrated by these people.

And two of the people responsible were in his control at the moment. But he also knew it was not enough to deal with them for past actions. He needed to get the details of the planned and future attacks on Tango Section. Then he could find a way to neutralize or stop these people and their attacks entirely. It was critical in many ways and truly a matter of national security.

More On How We Got Here

Travis had heard the political arguments and understood the political imperatives of the recent past. These had driven policy decisions and they had driven the Carter Administration in their quest to conquer the high ground of space. He also knew the advantages and he had benefited directly and personally from the capabilities of this high tech international competition.

It had all become a sort of emerging high tech war in which they were all engaged. But, dedicated men and women still risked their lives every day in a deadly activity here on earth. Here on earth is where people died horrible deaths from assassins and explosions. All the satellites in the world could still not see into a man's heart.

That had been the problem; in a world of limited federal budgets and political imperatives, cuts had to be made. And the Administration had made the hard choices as they had cut the funding for the Human Intelligence arms and capabilities of several agencies. That was how they had found much of the money to build and launch the satellites and the other intelligence assets into service. The one exception, and the one carrot held out to the opposition and "doom-sayers," was that Tango Section would continue to function. It would function and it would be funded to do the mission, which was now much more narrowly defined.

But for all of its autonomy, authority and power, Tango Section was a fairly small group of dedicated individuals who risked everything to accomplish the missions they were given. Granted they were also given extreme latitude to get the job done but they were not in a comfortable office in DC reading reports and spreadsheets. And right now someone had been killing them one at a time and planned to kill more. In that world Julie had almost been collateral damage and he was dealing with the personal attack as well as he could.

Travis looked over and saw Ervin put the cutting tool onto the first knuckle of Farouq'a trigger finger and start to exert pressure. But then he stopped and stood up straight again taking the device away and waving it around as he spoke and continued to speak in Farsi. Farouq was sweating and looked very pale, and Travis wondered how many times Ervin had performed this little ploy. He let Farouq feel the cold steel and the pressure but then stopped and continued to talk making sure Farouq understood this could go on all day and all night. Then he did something a little different.

Ervin stepped across the small room to a table where there were laid out a variety of cutting tools and he laid the pliers on the table and picked up a pair of tailor's scissors. Continuing his monologue in Farsi he walked over to the bound and gagged man who was strapped to the chair. His arms were bound to the arms of the wooden chair and so were his hands giving easy access to his fingers, several of which had little nicks in the skin. This was likely from the repetition of the little drama Travis had seen play out as he had entered the room.

Ervin kept talking in Farsi as he leaned over and started cutting up the seams of Farouq's pants legs until the cloth hung loose and disconnected. Then he reached over and pulled away the remainder of the cloth that had once been a pair of pants. Farouq still sat there securely bound to the chair but his genitals were exposed and the look on his face now was one of absolute terror. Ervin crossed slowly to the little table again and laid the scissors back in their place.

Then Ervin picked up a small chef's torch and lit the flame. Farouq watched Ervin and his eyes got even bigger as the realizations played out in his mind. Ervin approached and held the torch down to make sure Farouq could feel the heat on his most private parts. The look on Ervin face would have been enough to frighten most people and it had the desired effect on Farouq.

Travis was about to step in to stop Ervin, because they were not here to torture people. They were after information, but he stopped in his tracks because Farouq began to talk. More precisely he began to make sounds through the gag in his mouth. Ervin looked over his shoulder at Tavis but did not move the torch away from their captive's crotch. Away from Farouq's field of vision Ervin winked and Travis came forward.

Of course, to be completely accurate, Ervin could have held up a large placard sign and Farouq would not have seen it. Farouq was not looking anywhere except down at his crotch, and at the torch just inches away, and he was sweating more profusely. Travis crossed behind the captive and loosened the gag. Farouq coughed twice and spat, then started talking rapidly in English to Travis, "Stop this madman and I will tell you all you want to know."

Travis made a show of holding up a warning hand to Ervin who feigned disappointment and barely controlled anger. But Ervin did not move from Farouq's field of vision and, while he did extinguish the flame on the small torch, he did not put the cooking tool down. He just held it at his side and glared at Farouq.

Over the next 45 minutes Farouq told the details of everything he was involved in with Alfred. Travis knew the whole thing was being recorded because he had triggered the switch as he crossed to remove Farouq's gag. The whole of Farouq's comments would be transmitted to Sheila and Bob, minus the preparation details before Farouq started talking. It was telling and it was in more detail than they could have hoped for.

When it was clear that Farouq had nothing more of substance to offer, Travis started to head to the door and made a show of clicking off the recorder. Farouq called out in terror, "Wait, I have told you everything you wanted to know. Do not leave me alone with this madman!"

Travis stopped and turned to face Farouq then speaking in Farsi Travis said, "But you have not told him what he most wants to hear." Farouq turned white as Ervin lit the torch again. Travis continued, "Perhaps you should ask his forgiveness for torturing him and humiliating him in front of his wife and daughter, who you also treated so cruelly."

Farouq started pleading and apologizing and begging for forgiveness. Ervin stopped and clicked the recording switch on again, "Say that all again please. I want it clear for my wife and daughter to hear." Then he waved the torch from the other side of the room and Farouq started again sounding very sincere as he begged for their forgiveness also and praising the courage of Ervin those many years ago.

Travis walked out and back to the other room where Alfred was also going into more detail than anyone expected as well. And the interrogator was writing as well as running a voice and video recorder. He waved to Travis to enter but held a finger to his lips for quiet. He clearly did not want to stop the flow of the confessions. Travis stood quietly and listened and made his own mental recording of everything that Alfred said.

Then as the stream of words began to dry up Travis caught the eye of the interrogator and silently mouthed, "Svetlana."

The interrogator did not miss a beat as he transitioned to the new topic. "Now, tell me about your executive assistant, the woman named Svetlana, is she a good Russian?"

"Oh, yes." Alfred said through slurred speech. Then he praised her work ethic and her basic intelligence and told how she was running a successful smuggling operation right under the American's noses. He had already praised her to his superiors and had big plans for her in the future. And then he added, "In fact today I have her escorting and assisting the Lady Sonja who is a hero of the revolution, as she makes the final preparation for our next big project."

Travis mimed, "Thank you!" to the interrogator and eased his way out of the room to contact Sheila on a secure phone.

As he left the room he heard the interrogator say, "Tell me about this next big project. Was it your idea?"

Chapter 20: Game On

The yellow phone rang on Sheila's desk and the room went dead quiet. "This is Sheila." She said into the instrument.

The voice on the other end was one she recognized, "Got what you need?"

"Oh, yes." She responded to Trav's query. Then she quickly added, "Oh, and your little smuggler, is the real deal. I plan to keep the case myself."

"Really?" the Travis said.

"Yes. I am sure she can be turned and may wind up as the local representative replacing her boss given what is about to happen." Sheila said cryptically.

"Well, this is not just a social call, I need to get those details ASAP for my own planning. If you can." Travis said.

"Yes, that file is just finished and if you ignore the typos we won't bother to proof read it before sending the file on to you." As she said those words on the line that was on a speaker in the room, a team of three analysts and an admin person were compiling the final draft. They all looked up as if she had thrown a bucket of cold water onto their table. Sheila saw their reaction and added to the caller but so the rest of the room could hear, "The substantive data will be accurate but don't hold us to the 'happy to glad' fine tuning that might be necessary. We will mark the pages as working papers."

Travis said quickly, "I don't care how you mark it, I just need the data to I can get moving. I suspect the deadline is looming."

"Indeed it is, my friend. You will have what we have immediately. Now, let me go and make good on that promise."

"OK." Travis replied, "Thanks for everything. See you when I am done."

Alfred And Farouq

A package of very compromising photos was being delivered by diplomatic pouch to the US Mission in Berlin so that they could forward it to their East German interlocutor. That fellow would pass it along to the Russians with a request that it be opened only by the Chief of FSI in Dresden. Before the day was over Vladimir Putin would be looking at very graphic and compromising photos of Alfred and Farouq cavorting together with three prostitutes.

But that would be later today and right now Alfred did not know any of that yet. He knew his head hurt and he knew he was naked and that was odd because he did not normally sleep naked. As he began to move and stretch in an attempt to clear his head he had vague memories of something disjointed and disconnected maybe a bad dream. Then suddenly, he sat up ramrod straight in bed and looked down. He was indeed naked and he knew that someone had put him to bed. Then the full realization came streaming into is consciousness.

Of course someone had put him to bed, it was two of the women. "What women?" Alfred asked an empty room as another flash of memory came into his consciousness. He had been interrogated yesterday and now he was in a room; no, he was in his bedroom and Farouq was in the living room. Wait! Farouq?

Alfred stumbled across the bedroom and threw wide the door that opened onto his living room. He started to have vague memories of Farouq and the three women. Three women? There were no women here. Where was Farouq? Alfred stumbled further into the room from his bedroom, Farouq was on the couch.

Farouq was equally naked and the room was full of the evidence of a drunken party, no not a party, a drunken orgy. He was leaning over Farouq's still unconscious form trying to wake him when the door flew open. The room was suddenly filled with people pointing cameras and asking questions.

The most dominant question was, "Where is the girl?" Alfred asked, "What girl?" just as Farouq was starting to awaken. He rolled to one side and threw up onto the carpet. "The girl you two old perverts hurt last night. You know, the girl who was tied and hit and left with a bloody nose, when the other two girls made their escape. Where is she?" The reporter was almost screaming.

And Svetlana

Meanwhile, Svetlana was waking to an empty room with a split lip, and a bruised face, as well as several bruises on her torso. She touched each of the injuries and smiled, she had never been so happy. Svetlana liked Sheila, the American woman had arrived in the night in a private plane. She was some sort of official and a friend of the American man who had first caught her setting up the little smuggling ring.

Just then the American woman came into the room carrying a cup of steaming coffee. She held the coffee out to Svetlana and said, "Here, I thought you might be ready for a cup."

"Yes, I am." Svetlana answered Sheila.

"So how are the bruises?" Sheila asked.

"Well I can tell where they are without using a mirror so they must be about right." Svetlana said.

"I am truly sorry about that," Sheila said, "but later today everyone has to believe you were injured trying to save Sonja. And they have to believe that you fought to keep her alive and got yourself injured in the process. We will take you to the safe house very soon and make sure everything is as it should be. Then you will 'discover the body' and make the call to your superiors in Bonn, Berlin and Moscow, and follow their instructions before calling the police."

Svetlana nodded and Sheila continued, "Save the call to Dresden for last. We want to be up on line and able to intercept all those calls. That sequence of calls will help us identify exactly what role Dresden is playing in the whole business and where exactly Putin fits into the hierarchy." Sheila reviewed the script and Svetlana nodded in understanding. She was also interested to know exactly what role the asshole from Dresden would play in her future but she doubted the Americans would share what they found out.

The American woman, Sheila, had arrived on a non-scheduled flight last night from Spain. That is what the interrogator, Janet, had told her would happen. And both of the American women had been honest in their dealings and in making sure she knew exactly what would happen. They were right too, if she managed to pull this off, she would be a hero of the fatherland and well on her way to becoming known, in a good way, inside her agency."

Svetlana knew this game was a dangerous one, but so was everything else in her life. She had away been "working without a net" ever since she had realized she was in a girls' orphanage so many years ago. Her choice in this career had not been without risk and she had developed the ability to tell when something "felt like it might work" and she had that feeling now. She raised her Tee shirt and looked at herself in the mirror.

Her eye was bruised and her lip was split and there were two large bruises on her right side and one on her left side. It did indeed look very convincing but most convincing was the flesh wound on her upper arm where the bullet had grazed her arm. It had hurt like crazy when the fellow had done it but she had to admit now that it made the whole thing very convincing. And the one-handed bandage they had instructed her how to do this morning made it all the more believable.

Sonja And Heinrich

While Svetlana was being beaten by a very apologetic young man; and while Farouq and Alfred were having their "sex party" Sonja and Heinrich were sitting down to chat in another part of town. "Please sit and relax." Sonja said to Heinrich who had always been her lead thug when she needed dirty work done, "I have fresh coffee if you would like a cup."

"Yes, please. That would be very nice after that trip I have just finished." Heinrich replied and continued, "I am sorry I could not finish the assignment. Would you like me to try again?"

Sonja poured a cup and brought it over to where Heinrich was sitting and handed it to him. "No, I think we will have our best chance in the course of the next project at the tennis match." Heinrich nodded and as she sat she added, "I do appreciate you finishing that business with Hansel. He had become too much of a liability."

"Listen, I want to return the money for this one because I did not finish the job. And, I must tell you that finally getting rid of Hansel was almost a pleasure!" they both chuckled at this little joke and Heinrich continued, "But, while the explosion worked to bring his woman out of the house, she fell and I missed the shot."

Sonja cut him off with a wave of her hand, "No, my old friend, that was not your error. The woman fell, and over that you had no control, besides we still have the next opportunity coming very soon."

The knock at the door interrupted them and they looked at each other both questioning with their eyes. Sonja started to rise to answer the door but Heinrich waved her to stay seated and stood himself. "I will send them away." Then as he crossed to the door the knock came again.

Ervin stood in front of the door with Travis out of the door's peephole sightline and with his back against the adjoining wall. As Heinrich opened the door Ervin was raising his fist to knock again but he lowered his hand and said, "Your delivery is here." Then he stepped aside quickly and Travis replaced him in the door's opening.

Heinrich recognized Travis immediately and reached for the weapon holstered behind his back. In the time it took him to move Travis fired his silenced pistol and shot Heinrich twice in the chest. The he stepped quickly over the body to enter the room as Ervin dragged Heinrich's lifeless corpse back into the room and closed the door. Sonja tried to stand as she reached for her own weapon.

Travis wrenched the gun out of her hand and backhanded her across the face causing her to fell back into her chair, as she almost growled, "You."

Travis looked at her a moment and then said slowly, "You have one chance to live and that is to tell me all there is to know about your next attack."

"Go to hell. We should have killed you five years ago when I drugged you and brought you to the hotel room to die." Sonja said through gritted teeth.

"You are such a failure because I am still alive and you sent these idiots to kill my girlfriend and she is alive. In fact it appears that you have only succeeded in killing one of your own, Hansel." Travis could see that his words were striking a nerve, "So, last chance, tell me everything or die right here right now."

"Go to hell! I will tell you nothing!" Sonja growled through clenched teeth.

"You know what, I believe you." Travis raised his silenced pistol and put a bullet between her eyes. The force of the impact drove her head back against the chair.

Travis turned to Ervin and said simply, "We are done here." The two men left the scene that Svetlana would see in a short while when she was to start her career as a "hero of the fatherland."

The two of them quickly pulled the little microphones from their hiding places confident they had all they needed on tape already. They left the scene, walking slowly as if on a stroll as Ervin asked, "Why did we kill her without getting any information?"

"We already have the information we need, Ervin." Travis responded. "That information came from Farouq and Alfred. And the fellow we shot first was to have been one of the attackers to finish what any of the other attackers might be unable to finish."

"So, you were playing with her?" Ervin asked.

"No. If she had given any indication of being willing to cooperate then I would have called the interrogation team. But this woman tried once before to kill me. She gave the order to shoot my woman. And she did not give any indication that she might cooperate so I followed my orders."

"I see." Ervin said and the matter was closed as far as he was concerned.

The Next Moves

Very shortly they would pick Svetlana up and drop her at Sonja's house where she would "wake up" after being drugged, beaten and shot resisting the western agents as she was trying to save Sonja's life. But she would "discover" Sonja's body, and the body of Sonja's associate, this morning when she came to. Then she would start calling her superiors for instructions after she was "unable to reach Alfred" at his home or his office. And of course by midday she would receive the "package."

The package would have compromising photos of Alfred and Farouq as well as three women engaged in sex acts of different sorts. That would be her second round of calls to Moscow asking for instructions and proposing that she send the photos immediately in order to get the information to her supervisor in Moscow. And yes, she would fax them first and follow up with the real thing as soon as the diplomatic pouch left.

Then she would call a third time asking for someone to come immediately to take charge on the spot when Alfred was taken into police custody about the time the tabloid papers started to run the story about a Russian, Iranian Sex Circle. It would be too late and she would have to be the representative for the Russian diplomatic service.

Sonja who had been killed with a bullet between the eyes and Svetlana had been wounded and beaten and both were clearly heroes of the state. Fortunately, although Sonja had died in the attack, Svetlana had only been grazed by a bullet from the attackers. She had survived and she was alive. She would alert Moscow that she was trying desperately to get word out to the three teams.

Of course Sheila was with her as she made the calls to her superiors and helped tutor her through the notifications. But Sheila had to leave her side because the wild card came in the form of a Russian member of the Security Service who drove down from Bonn to talk with her.

Some FSB representative, a distinguished former KGB Officer was coming from Dresden in East Germany but that would take about six to eight hours. Svetlana was finally going to meet Putin. She looked forward to telling him just how much Alfred hated him and what Alfred had said about him every time they had ended a phone call.

Chapter 21: Tennis Anyone

"All I have to say is, this better be right." Emilio said looking over at Travis.

"Well, my friend, this is the data the team put together from those long interviews with Farouq and Alfred." Tavis responded and Ervin shook his head agreeing with Travis.

"And tell me again what it is you need from me." Emilio did not sound happy.

"Emilio, I really don't know. But Sheila says you guys have the best tech available and that your people are the best at what they do. So, just bug and snoop on all the electrons you can find." Travis said looking over at Emilio who was definitely not happy about everything.

"I understand the concern, but consider that Alfred and Farouq have been burned with their people. Hansel, Heinrich and Sonja are dead; and we have learned about a new player in the game in Dresden. He, however, will be a problem for another day because we don't have the assets to go after him right now. And more importantly we do not have approval to go after him right now. Svetlana is groomed and placed to provide us information for a long, long time. And we know the last of their teams are coming here to kill Jason, Faye, and Eric. We only have to stop these three hits. What's not to like abut this plan?" Travis said.

"Travis, I get it," Emilio started again, "this thing has been in play a long time and there is great propaganda value to pulling another couple of high profile defectors away from the Soviet Union. And I know that Tango #2, Tango #4, and Tango #7 are coming here anyway for just that purpose. But helping an athlete defect and stopping assassins are two very different things! They don't even go in the same job jar!"

Travis was starting to speak but Emilo, who was on a roll, kept going, "This is the International German Open and it has been played in the Rothenbaum since 1892. Travis, there are several public access transport methods, and that alone is a surveillance nightmare. And there are all the parking areas, and vehicle staging areas for short term waiting, not to mention the casual tourists coming to visit the lake. Look, Hamburg is no 'out of the way' sleepy little German hamlet!" And the hotels are scattered and numerous."

Travis interjected, "So figure out how you would do it and start with surveillance on those routes. We have everyone in the same hotel so that should be the target for the assassins. And, I promise you that everybody on our team will wear a wire if that makes it easier. But you need to get busy because they will start arriving almost any moment now."

Emilio knew when he was beaten and he knew there was no easy way out of this whole thing. He shrugged and nodded and started to turn away when Travis stopped him, "Emilio, I understand but we just do not have an option. There are teams out there trying to kill our people and they have been successful more than once already. This is our chance to shut down this current threat once and for all by taking out the last of their teams already in the field. I can't think of any group of people I would rather have on our side than you and your techs."

That seemed to re-inflate Emilio, at least a bit, and he responded, "We will do everything we can. I promise you that."

"That is all I can ask for." Travis said in response and they parted company.

The Operatives

The three operatives of Tango Section, in question, knew they were being targeted but so was every operative in the organization and the work must go on. So Faye Smithfield was headed to Germany to try her luck on the clay courts of Am Rothenbaum in Hamburg. Faye and her husband, Tom Smithfield, always travelled together and he served as her trainer and coach, as well as part time manager. The agency definitely got a "two for one" deal with the Smithfields. What was not commonly known about the ruggedly handsome and very fit Tom Smithfield is that he was also a retired US Navy SEAL and an experienced combat veteran.

They were one of several professional players arriving for a series of exhibition matches at this historically famous tennis club. And modern day interest in tennis had grown exponentially every since the 1980 German Open Championship. It had been a men's Tennis Tournament that was a part of the Super Series of the 1980 Grand Prix Circuit from the 12th to the 18th of May of that year. The overall winner of this 72nd competition had been an American, Harold Solomon.

All of that was interesting but the real reason for Tango #4, Faye Smithfield, had to do with her incredible reflexes and physical skills that were the envy of all. But Faye and Tom were also really there because there was a high probability of a defection from a former Soviet Bloc nation state. The pattern for this sort of activity had been set, in 1975. At the young age of 18, Martina Navratilova, had asked the United States for political asylum and was granted temporary residence. Navratilova had become a US citizen in 1981 and it had all made the news again.

The sports world was in as much upheaval as the international political world. This was especially so with the 1984 Olympics just finished. And of course a kind of part two set for 1985, defections were a political prize to be sought and exploited. But the whole thing became embroiled in Olympic Boycotts at national level in the USA. And of course, other nations responded in kind along the lines of political ideology.

And that set of conditions gave cover to Tango #2, a guy named Ellerbe. Jason Ellerbe, former US Army Captain, and Travis Lemon, former US Air Force Captain, had served many of the same places at the same time; but had not known each other back then. Ellerbe was at the tournament posing as a reporter with a wire service.

The 1984 Winter Olympics had been nicknamed "Sarajevo '84" in the sports media and was a winter multi-sport event held from the 8th to the 19th of February of that year. The venue for this historic event was Sarajevo, Bosnia and Herzegovina, Yugoslavia. It had been the first winter Olympics in a socialist state and the first in a Slavic language nation.

Politically, Russia had counted this as a propaganda victory since it followed the 1980 Moscow Summer Olympics of the Soviet Union so closely.

This would, unfortunately for the world, be short-lived as the region was destined to break into a brutal ethno-conflict in 1992. All the wins by athletes, and all the renovation of the infrastructure, would be destined to be destroyed by the warring factions as the region came apart at the ethnic seams. Some rebuilding would be attempted after the conflict but twenty years later many of the iconic locations, like the bobsled and luge track, would still remain abandoned.

And of course all this movement of athletes and their gear, as well as the news media and their gear, meant a robust group of porters and maintenance men. And of course this meant there would be the "expediters" who could quietly make things happen in the background. And that is where Tango #7 came into the gathering. His name was Eric Jones and he was by all accounts the most physically powerful man Trav had ever met. But he was not a body builder who spent his time in a gym. The guy had come by his muscles the hard way.

Eric Jones looked more like a dockworker or a furniture deliveryman. On a bet one night he had lifted a sofa by himself and moved it from one room to another without breaking a sweat. He was a large black man, physically imposing, and he exuded charm. He also affected a demeanor of always being very polite and absolutely invisible in plain sight. As previously noted, he had been a college instructor on track for a full professorship when he had made the career change to covert ops.

Eric was by academic training a political scientist. But he had come to realize that political science in a college environment is less personally rewarding that a hands on approach putting theory into practice. Let the academics on the left continue their "talk-shop" activities; he would be changing things in a "hands on" way.

The entire group was a bit nervous as the sports event began and they all had their sensors out. This initiative after all, had interest all the way to the

White House. So they knew it was important; and they knew it was personally dangerous for each of them individually and collectively. But what they did not know is if there was only one hit team or three, or maybe even more with a back-up team deployed in case one of the other teams was a failure. No one would breath easy until it was all over and they were alone having a glass of wine together someplace.

They also knew there was a distinct advantage as the hit teams so far had known who their targets were and what they looked like. Meanwhile the targets, specifically the operatives themselves, did not know what the hit teams looked like. They did know that Travis was joining them and that helped because it did help even the playing field. Of course he was also the target of an unknown killer himself.

Chapter 22: First Volley

Travis arrived at their hotel, near the club in Hamburg, in a hired Mercedes Benz, as in fact most of the guests and spectators did. He was travelling as Harry, Melon, an oil executive on vacation from the ARAMCO's Home Offices in Saudi Arabia. The hotel was one of the nicer ones of the three hundred plus in Hamburg. The brochure he held also noted there were over forty tennis court facilities in and around Hamburg. There were indoor venues, like the one he would be attending but there were also outdoor venues, like schools and private clubs as well as public tennis courts.

Harry placed the brochure in his jacket pocket as the driver opened his door. He exited the vehicle slowly taking in his surroundings and spotting Eric Jones. Jones had appeared as if by magic and looked to be heading up a group of bellhops and baggage carriers. Eric and Harry made eye contact and Eric came over immediately.

"Mr. Harry Melon?" the large black man asked in a

very smooth voice.

"Yes, and you are?" Travis, in his Harry Melon persona, responded.

"My name, sir, is Eric Jones but everyone just calls me 'Jonsey.' And if there is anything my team or I can do to make your stay more pleasant please do not hesitate to call." Eric held out a small envelope and handed it to Harry Melon. "I have taken the liberty of checking with reservations and you will find your key inside this package. The room number is written on the outside and my personal contact information is also inside."

Harry took the envelope and passed Eric a fifty-dollar tip that he noticed caught the eye of the two young bellhops already getting his luggage from the trunk of the vehicle. Harry started to turn away when Eric raised a large black hand in a sort of wave to stop him and said, "With the international nature of the coming days, if you need help, I also speak German and French as well as English."

"Thank you, Jonsey. That is helpful." Then almost as if suddenly realizing he had a question Travis stopped and turned back to Eric who stood a little straighter immediately in response. Harry Melon asked, "Jonsey, do you know if the lady named Faye Smithfield made it for the exhibition matches? I do like the way she plays."

"Yes, sir." Eric said immediately, "I saw her earlier with her manager. They were with that sports writer, Jason Ellerbe. She seemed to be giving him an interview. I could look up their suite number and get the information to you, if you like.

"Yes, actually her contact information would be helpful, I hope to ask her for an autograph for my niece while I am here." Then shifting gears as if to dismiss Jonsey, Travis said, "If you could, please get that information to me when you can. I really need to get to my room and unpack."

Eric gave a little half bow from the waist and signaled the baggage handlers to get Harry Melon's luggage to his suite.

Half an hour later, there was a knock on Harry Mellon's door and he opened it to see Jonsey.

"I have that information you requested, sir."

Jonsey said as Harry opened the door to let him inside the suite of rooms.

The large black man with the broad shoulders stepped forward, waited for the room door to close and stepped forward. Then almost face-to-face and towering over Travis, Jonsey hugged the smaller man. And Travis hugged him back. "Damn!" Travis said with a broad smile, "It is good to see you again, my friend."

"Good to see you too, Trav!" Eric Jones said warmly. Then as they broke the hug and took a seat to chat Jonsey asked, "So, what do you know that we do not know?"

Travis took a deep breath as he started to answer the big man's question. "Remember that incident I had with the stewardess who almost took me out a few years back?" Jonsey nodded and Trav continued, "Well her name was Sonja and she is now dead with one between the eyes. But she was the field ops officer for a Soviet-Russia sanctioned effort to eliminate most, if not all, of the operatives of Tango Section." They were interrupted by another knock on the door.

Travis went to answer the door as Faye and Tom steamrolled past him followed by Jason. There were hugs and greetings all around and as all sat Tavis said, "Sheila and the 'old man' would shit if they knew we were all together in the same room in the field. You know, this would make one hell of a target."

"Well," Faye said in a soft conspiratorial voice, "let's not tell them shall we?"

"Besides," Tom interjected, "this is likely the only time we will be able to do this anyway. So spill! Tell us everything."

"As I was telling Jonsey, that stewardess who almost took me out a few years back was running a sort of field op to take out the operatives. The whole thing is Russian and Soviet sanctioned, with plausible deniability set through the Cultural attaché in Frankfurt. We have him compromised and interrogated and set up with compromising pictures."

"Ooh, I like dirty picture ops." Faye said hugging Tom's arm." Jason just rolled his eyes and looked at the ceiling.

Tom replied, "You guys do know she just does that to get a reaction."

"Yes, we know!" Jason and Jonsey said in unison.

Travis tried to regain control of the conversation again, as he cleared his throat and said, "There was another 'bad guy' with Alfred, the Russian agent. His name is Farouq and he is IRGC and we have him in the same pictures. A set is also in the mail to his leadership in Iran so they should take him out for us. And with luck the handlers in Moscow will take out Alfred and replace him." They all nodded and Jonsey started to ask a question but Travis stopped him with a finger wave to wait, "But the real prize is we now have a mole inside that office and that is how we managed to put a hole in Sonja's head right between her eyes."

"Sonja?" Jason asked.

"Oh, sorry I made that linkage before you guys all showed up." Tavis said, "Sonja, the old stewardess I tangled with a few years back, was the field ops director for this whole thing."

"OK." Jason said, "I got it. Moscow sanctioned this

series of attacks, and Alfred and Farouq worked the strategy while Sonja was the tactical level dirty work, right?"

"See, you're not as dumb as you sound in that sports column you do as part of your cover." Faye said.

"I will have you know that is not just a cover!" Jason protested, I actually have a readership! And just wait until you see how I report our little interview earlier, lady."

Faye shot him a look that said volumes.

And Tavis interjected, "Focus, focus!" As everyone settled back enjoying the little banter, Travis continued. "Problem is we don't know everything we need to know."

"Do we ever?" Jason interjected.

Travis ignored that comment and continued, "We do know the one guy who has been working with Sonja for years was named Heinrich, he was the one who I stabbed in the previous incident with Sonja and he was the one who shot Julie trying to kill her." Travis opened the folder and passed a photo around.

"I assume you killed the bastard!" Faye said and then added in a different tone, "How is Julie? I think I speak for everyone of us when I say that incident had us all praying for your girlfriend." The rest of the small group murmured agreement and passed the photo around. "Well I see you did." Faye said again when the picture of a very dead Heinrich was passed to her.

Travis continued, "Everyone we have seen him talking to in the past is a suspect and Emilio and his people are scanning the old surveillance forage looking for his face. And in their spare time they are watching us. That is where you are so critical, Jonsey."

"OK." Jonsey said, "Do we have photos of the other shooters or at least who we believe them to be?"

"Yes," Travis passed around more photos with a short blurb about each one. Then he wrapped up his comments. "But not all of them are shooters. That first guy likes poisons and likes to inject his victims in a crowd. He just walks up and sticks a needle in someone's stomach and disappears in the crowd."

"Lovely fellow." Faye said sarcastically.

Travis continued, "The next guy is a shooter but

favors close shots with a small caliber silenced weapon. And you know Heinrich was a long distance shooter so we suspect there is likely another sniper out there as his backup. The last guy likes to strangle his victims with a piano wire garrote but is also known to use a knife or even a sword once or twice."

Travis could see the effect this was having on his colleagues but they needed to know what they were up against. "And, Sheila suspects at least one backup assassin maybe with a bomb."

"A bomb?" Faye spoke up.

Travis answered her, "That projection came from Wallis and the technical intelligence guys based on some communications intercepts. So, that leaves us with four to six assassins and no idea which one of them is coming after which one of us. Like I said, Jonsey is critical to all of us right now, and I assume each of you have your own discreet communications back to Sheila and our boss?" There were head nods all around.

Game On

Then Travis broke out a bottle of wine and asked,

"Everyone up for a toast to our success. And I mean catching a defector to embarrass the Soviets, while stopping them from killing any of us." Everyone nodded agreement and Trav poured as each raised their glass to toast victory and a safe return for everyone at the end of the mission. Trav's gut told him that they would not have long to wait but he did not expect the first attempt right then, at that precise moment in time.

As they were setting down the glasses, the room door behind them, the same door through which they had all come, flew open slamming against the wall, and a man ran in with a silenced gun in each hand. No words were spoken, and no warning was given. He was just firing at close range. The first bullet hit Tom in the back of the arm and instinctively he dove for cover across the room, hitting the floor and rolling back to his feet but trailing blood from his left bicep.

The gunman turned to Faye but she was already gone in the opposite direction that Tom had chosen and the shot went wild. Next the gunman shifted to point one of his weapons at Jason but, before he could pull the trigger again, Jonsey had lifted an end table and shoved it into the fellow's ribs pinning him to the wall. Everyone heard the wood cracking and ribs breaking as the fellow grunted and then bellowed from the pain and lost consciousness.

Travis moved quickly to his luggage and pulled out a wound kit and tossed it to Faye who caught it in midair as she crossed the room to check on her husband. Tom Smithfield was taking it all in stride, and the room became silent as Jason said simply. "Looks like the one who likes to work up close and personal with a small caliber pistol, except he brought two of them this time. I am guessing he was not expecting to find so many of us in here at one time."

"You are probably right, but he is not going anywhere and let's make sure Tom is OK then we will deal with him." Travis said and turning to Jonsey he added, "Nice move there Jonsey! Did you learn that in a Kung Fu class?"

"No, I saw it on a kid's cartoon show." Jonsey replied.

Even Tom laughed at that one, at least until Faye

pushed the needle into his wound with the antibiotic. "Looks like a minor wound," she said, "and it went all the way through. Good dose of antibiotic and a couple of stitches and he will be good as new."

"Faye, need any help over there?" Travis asked.

Tom spoke up immediately, "You think I am going to let any of you Neanderthals do this? Not on your life, I trust Faye a lot more than I trust you guys. Nothing personal." He added at the end.

"No offense taken." Jason answered for the group.

"What do you think we ought to do with him?" Jonsey asked the group at large.

"Just keep him pinned to the floor a few more minutes, I got this covered." Travis said, adding, "Already called my buddy in GSG9 and they have some help standing by, after all terror on German soil is their thing."

Just then there was a rush of activity at the door as a medic with a gurney came in followed by a med tech and a couple or armed members of the Border Guards Group Nine Counter Terror Unit, known as GSG9. The med tech looked at the gunmen with no sympathy in his eyes, "I assume this is the intruder?"

"Yes, sir." Jonsey said, "I think I messed up his timing when I forced him to let go of his guns. Oh, and I heard wood cracking and what sounded like a couple of ribs snapping as well."

"OK. Got it." The med tech said asking, "But did you say guns? Plural?"

"Yes." Jason jumped into the exchange. "Here they are." He said as he handed them over to the agent by the barrels, presenting the grips to the man.

"Nice." The agent said, "Pretty fancy with the silencers made into the barrel. Professional equipment; you guys were lucky."

The med tech was over kneeling beside Faye and looking at her work on Tom, "Pretty good field dressing, lady." He said with a degree of admiration in his voice.

Trav's friend, Hans Feldman, came in next, placed his hands on his hips and looked around taking in the scene, "So, Trav, is this how it is going to be for the whole tournament? I was hoping to sit quietly and watch some world class tennis!"

Travis stepped forward, extended his hand and then pulled Hans in for a hug, "Brother, am I glad to see you!"

"Put me down, asshole, I am trying to project an air of command with quiet confidence here. Besides my men are watching." Hans said pushing Travis away.

"And can I say just how manly you look, Herr Major!" Faye said.

Then Tom joined the discussion affecting a look of concern, "I see how you are, one little scratch and you ignore me and start flirting with the European guy."

Hans turned to face the lady and the wounded man, "And, you are the exhibition player scheduled for tomorrow, Faye Smithfield! It is an honor, and you must be her husband, Tom Smithfield. May I say, sir, that I have had the pleasure of reading some of your classified reports from your days as a US Navy SEAL and they are impressive!" Then turning to Jason, he added, "And that would make you the sports writer, Jason Ellerbe." Hans said extending his hand.

"You have no idea how much we appreciate you and your team here. The response time was incredible!" Jason said, then mentally switching gears he asked, "Can I use any of this in a news story?"

"Yes." Hans said simply, then clearing his throat, "A deranged Chechen terrorist attacked the international tennis star Ms. Faye Smithfield and her husband in an attempt to make a political statement about the conflict in his country. Our heart-felt apologies go out to Ms. Smithfield and her husband, a former USN Officer who sustained a slight wound fending off the attacker. Ms. Smithfield and her husband, who now works as her manager and trainer, declined further comment."

"Chechen?" Travis said with a note of incredulity in his voice.

"Well, he could have been." Hans said shrugging and then back to Jason and holding up a finger as if warning a child, "No mention of GSG9 for now! I am serious. We do not want to tip our hand. It will all come out soon enough. The credit for now goes to resort security and the local Polizie."

Jason shrugged in a gesture of surrender but said aloud, "I can work with that."

"I hate to break up this little love fest but we need to separate and get out there to counter these threats." Jonsey said.

"Quite right." Hans said and then with a little smile, "But you people really should pick your friends a little more carefully." Jerking a thumb towards Travis, "I have known this man for a while and trouble does seem to follow him around."

"Hans," Travis said in response, "thank you again." The two men shook hands as two workmen were already patching the bullet holes, cleaning things and resetting the furniture. In very short order it was as though it had never even happened. The group had dispersed; the GSG9 response team was gone, and Travis was alone with his thoughts. He opened a beer from a small refrigerator and wondered what Julie was doing right now.

Chapter 23: Next Move

"Sometimes there is no substitute for sheer luck!" Travis said softly to himself as he spotted the fellow at a table alone in the corner of the room with a spectacular sunrise to his back. "From that table the fellow would be practically invisible with the glare of the sunrise through the window behind him." Travis said to himself. Then a frown crossed his face, and if anyone had been watching they would have wondered what concern had crossed Trav's mind.

"That seating is exactly what I would have chosen." Travis said under his breath. He thought how it gave the fellow an excellent view of the entire dining room. But the diner had not spotted Travis, because Travis had come in from a side door. He had been chatting out of public view with Jason. The longer he was able to observe the fellow the more sure he was that this was one of their killers. The guy had tried to alter his appearance and he looked different from the picture, but there was no doubt in Trav's mind. This was the assassin who preferred the use of poison over guns.

Just following good tradecraft and being careful not to arouse any suspicion, Travis and Jason had not entered the dining room together. For for that matter they had not even been seen arriving together. Travis had come into the room from a side door off the kitchen and Jason had gone around to the main entrance. Jason had just come in and the fellow that Travis was observing had spotted Jason immediately; but still did not appear to have seen Travis. Even better was that the fellow did not seem to know he was being watched.

Again Travis said to himself softly, "Sometimes there is no substitute for sheer luck!" Travis pulled back into the narrow hallway that led to the kitchen and reached for a busboy's jacket hanging from a hook on the wall and slipped it on. Then he went again through the side door off the kitchen and, keeping his back to the fellow at the window. He walked straight to the table where Jason had just taken a seat.

Jason looked up with a question in his eyes as Travis busied himself adjusting the cutlery and dishes on the table, already perfectly set. Under his voice he said simply, "Target. Seated by the window. Poison-guy." Then he walked away quickly out the front of the dining room, slipped back around to the kitchen and disposed of his temporary disguise. Sometimes, he thought, the best hiding place is in the open. In a restaurant, waiters and busboys are mostly invisible, as he had just demonstrated.

Jason knew that the would-be assassin had already spotted him, and his defensive senses were onto high alert. He opted for the buffet just so he could move around the room going to and from the delicacies laid out along the hot bar and the cold bar. He had just filled his plate when he saw the target making his approach, obviously intending to take advantage of Jason at his most precarious with a plate full of food in his hands.

The fellow reached into one of the pockets in the front of his jacket. Jason saw the outline of his fist through the thin material and knew he was about to withdraw his hand, wrapped around a small cylinder, a syringe. Jason stepped forward with amazing speed dropping the plate as he yelled at the top of his voice, distracting the would-be assassin. The action also drew everyone's attention in the dining room. "Somebody call a doctor! This man is having a seizure!"

Simultaneously Jason's hands, now free, with food flying everywhere, ripped the man's hand out of his pocket and literally forced the syringe form the fellow. He jabbed the syringe into the man's arm through the fabric of his jacket. Jason said again loudly, "I have his medicine, I hope we are in time. Please somebody call a doctor, this man is having a seizure and does not look well!"

Then turning to the man directly and pulling the needle from the man's arm, he saw the look of terror on the man's face. "Sir, are you all right?" Jason said to the man as the light left his eyes. Amidst the confusion the flying food and other morning diners trying to get medical help, Jason was counting on people seeing what he wanted them to see. By most accounts, including Travis just coming in from the doorway, Jason was trying to help a man inject himself

315

as he had a deadly seizure. It was a real tragedy. Jonsey came in from his station out front and helped Jason get the man out, through the lobby and into the ambulance that was arriving.

Travis noticed that Hans was in the passenger seat of the ambulance, and he smiled at his old friend who shared his passion for getting "bad guys" off the street. By Trav's account that was two of the expected assassins. One had made an attempt on Faye and had wounded Tom in the process. Today the poison expert had gone after Jason and it was only his Guardian Angels who had prevented a disaster from unfolding. In a passing thought Travis tried to remember his last chat with Father Joe; maybe it was time to sit and chat with his favorite Priest.

Refocusing on the problem at hand, he knew from the intel, that Svetlana had helped them develop, that there were at least two more hits slotted against him and against Jonsey. And personally he still thought it only made sense that there would be a "fall back" assassin in case one or all of the others failed. That scenario, if Travis were right would lend itself to a weapon, like a bomb or gas, or something equally dangerous for larger groups of people. He would ask Hans to request a bomb team with a bomb-detection dog to be in or around the tennis club just for safety sake.

Chapter 24: Jonsey And Travis

Eric Jones, the man that everybody counted on in this operation was an unlikely hero. He had originally come off an impoverished farm in Alabama; and would likely have stayed on that same farm except for one very attentive physical education teacher. The teacher was also the High School Football Coach, and "Coach" liked to win. He had discovered that Jonsey could play football, so he placed Jonsey as a lineman because of his sheer size. Then one day just before practice began, Jonsey was warming up with the school quarterback who was his best friend.

The coach checked his watch and there were still a few minutes before he blew his whistle, to start the practice, so he let the boys continue warming up and horsing around. Besides it was good for them to all enjoy their time as a team. He had just brought the whistle to his lips as he moved to look over the field, he turned just in time to watch the two friends. Jonsey made an incredible catch of a very bad throw from the sometimes erratic quarterback.

"Whoa!" The Coach yelled, "Do that again."

The two boys repeated the process a dozen times with the coach yelling random changes and directions as they threw the ball and caught it. Jonsey seemed to be able to tell where the ball was going to be and when it was going to be there. He had that uncanny ability to predict where moving objects would land. Then as other team members began to just watch these two, the Coach started to put obstacles up to make it more difficult.

Two and then three of the teammates tried to close in on the two with aggressive harassing moves to interfere with the quarterback. Then the Coach added two or three of the fastest players closing in on Jonsey from different angles at the same time. He still made the catches with an amazing consistency. To make a long story short, that skill had paid his way to the college that would have been out of his reach otherwise. As it turned out his academic record at Tuscaloosa was as good or better than his sports record.

"Jonsey" applied for and was accepted into the

Political Science Department at Tuscaloosa on a graduate teaching assistantship. The flexible approach of the school administration, in a place that prides itself on its football program, meant that the teaching Jonsey assisted with was in the sports department. He helped refine the skills of receivers on the football team, he had so recently left when he had graduated. Two years later with an earned Doctorate to his credit, Jonsey got a job teaching at Auburn. It was a dream come true for a poor kid from a poor farm.

The rivalry between the two schools, Alabama which he had attended, and Auburn where he worked, swept him up into its embrace. He enjoyed the banter with his students and with his colleagues, especially during football season. Then it became automatic and a bit boring and Jonsey made a decision that changed his life. The more he read, the more he realized that our Founding Fathers may have been men of letters and reason and skilled at debates and logic; but they were also men of action. They founded a nation, not just with words and idea, but with actions. As his old coach would have said, "They had some skin in the game."

Skin In The Game

Dr. Eric Jones, PhD made a short trip down the road to the educational center of the USAF at Maxwell Air Force Base in Montgomery, Alabama. There he learned that the place is organized around the library and research facilities at the center of the "Academic Circle." All the professional military education schools and organizations are spaced around that focal point. There is an academic school for junior grade officers, one for mid-level officers and the Air Way College for Senior Officers. And there are resident advisors from other government agencies, like the Department of State, and the Central Intelligence Agency to name two of those represented.

There he learned that a young, very fit PhD, African-American was a desirable asset to recruiters from those agencies. And about a year later Jonsey left the other government agency facility at Langley, Virginia and headed into a field office in an unstable country in Africa. Ten years later that had led to him standing around, outside the hotel reception area, being invisible until someone needed something. He was the critical piece, the "pivot man" for this effort to facilitate a sports defection. The other part of the job was to simultaneously keep the members of Tango Section alive, literally.

Jonsey was swatting at an unseen bee, or something else, buzzing past his head when he heard a distant echo that sounded like a gunshot. He looked behind himself immediately and saw it. Jonsey turned and bent to inspect the hole behind him as another hole appeared off to one side barely missing his hand. Jonsey did not have to think, he just reacted. He dove to one side and scrambled behind cover even as his conscious mind recognized that his move to inspect the hole had likely saved his live as it caused the sniper to miss him with the second shot.

Then there was silence and he took a stealthy look over the shipping box behind which he was hiding. He breathed a sigh of relief immediately as his eyes focused in the distance. There on the ridge of a construction project in the distance, maybe a hundred and fifty yards away was Travis waving a cloth. Jonsey just shook his head in relief and disbelief.

How had he done that? Travis had gotten inside the head of the shooter and gone to the location from which he, Travis, would have made a shot. Then as Jonsey saw the lights and heard the distinct siren of the ambulance arriving at the location where Travis was, he knew the shooter was likely already dead. Jonsey shook his head, this was just one more example of Trav's gut instincts in the field.

Jonsey stood, smoothed his clothes and managed to make out Travis climbing into the back of the ambulance as it left the hilltop. Eric definitely had to go visit his favorite Church when this was all over. He needed to say a few prayers to Saint Michael for keeping him safe. Jonsey was not Catholic but he didn't believe in being rude to anybody's Saints. And since the Catholics had an Angel, Saint Michael, specifically charged to keep people safe, that sounded like a good idea to Jonsey!

Bombs

About an hour later an official looking van pulled

up to the front of the hotel and a young German Police Officer exited the vehicle and came directly to Jonsey. "Are you Eric Jones?" The man asked in German and then in English.

"I am," Jonsey answered in English and then in German and added, "How can I help you officer?"

I need to inform the management that we are gong to be doing a little search for safety reasons to ensure there are no explosives on the premises. This is our contribution to the tournament and we are doing courtesy inspections of several venues. Besides that way they can take credit with their guests for taking all precautions to preserve their guests safety and security."

"I understand completely," Jonsey said, "please come with me, officer."

Two hours later the Polizei had removed three suspicious bundles from the premises and into a special transport for further inspection. Two of the three had explosive devices in them and were detonated inside the transport vehicle. The third turned out to be some dirty laundry and a disassembled shotgun. The shotgun was returned to its owner who showed identification and a pass to his local shooting club.

Later In The Day

That evening, as people returned from the day's activities, the Polizei visit was presented as a precaution by a concerned hotel staff and the guests expressed praise for being so security minded. And, there was a reception for Faye Smithfield for her exhibition match with one of the young competitors from East Germany. The small-scale celebration was set for a corner of the main ballroom and Faye was hopeful that this might be the one to defect before the tournament was over.

As Travis entered the room, Faye and Tom were at the center of the action. Jason was playing the part of the sportswriter, with a camera dangling from a strap around his neck as he scribbled notes furiously in his little notebook. Jonsey was being invisible against the wall on one side of the room. He did however mouth a "Thank you." As he and Travis made eye contact.

Travis acknowledged the thanks from Jonsey with a nod and started to turn his attention to the center of the room. But he saw Jonsey's face change from thanks to alarm to anger in the blink of an eye. The big man was looking his way but not at him. Intuitively Travis knew he did not have the time to look behind himself so he reacted. He turned toward Jonsey and headed in his direction.

That was when he became aware of a presence off to one side and closing in his direction. Then something looped over his head and began to constrict around his neck. Travis managed to grab the wire with one hand and felt it cut into his fingers painfully. He struck out with his other hand trying to reach the man behind him but failed to land a solid blow. Travis began to fight for air amidst the pain in his neck and in his hand.

Travis kicked back savagely but only managed to make contact with a glancing blow off the heel of his shoe. As he started to feel things close in, he was aware of Jonsey talking to him in a loud voice and the pain began to stabilize. Then he realized he could breathe more easily. Jonsey twisted the short wooden handles of the garrote and began to remove it carefully from the canal it had already started to cut along one side of his neck. The other side of his neck, where his hand had been, was not nearly as badly cut and he began to think he might live after all.

"OK, Trav," Jonsey was saying, "I did my part. I killed the bastard; but you gotta' do your part and stay alive until the medics arrive." Travis did manage to look to one side and he saw the crumpled body of the assailant and he looked questioningly at Jonsey. Jonsey saw the look and added, "When you were trying to kick him I was picking him up, flipping him over and throwing him down on his head onto the floor. Broke his neck."

Travis was unable to speak as one medic placed an oxygen mask over his mouth while another bandaged his neck and a third was bandaging his hand. He could see Hans standing behind the medical team as he was hustled into a waiting ambulance. The next day an exclusive story would run with the byline of Jason Ellerbe describing his eyewitness account of the attack.

According to Jason, Mr. Harry Mellon, an oil executive on holiday from Saudi Arabia, was in Hamburg to enjoy the Tennis Tournament when an Iranian dissident attacked him. Thankfully the German GSG9 had been in the area double-checking hotel security. They had literally just walked into this particular hotel, which by the way had most excellent arrangements for the tournament participants, when the attack had taken place. Fortunately they were able to respond with medical first aid. Additionally, special thanks to a Mr. Eric Jones, a member of the hotel's security staff, for his quick reactions to tackle the assailant and pull him away from Mr. Mellon. The assailant did not survive the melee.

This is the second such incident at the hotel during the tournament and does not appear in any way related to the first involving tennis star Faye Smithfield who was giving an interview during a small gathering to congratulate her on her performance in the day's contests. The hotel management ensured everyone present, that they take security very seriously. The evidence of that is in both of these unrelated incidents no one was seriously hurt.

Mr. Mellon is being treated and has expressed his intentions to continue the healing and recovery process in the UK where he has some unfinished business to take care of. In other news two of the bright young superstars of tennis from behind The Wall have asked for asylum in West Germany and have expressed a desire to visit the United States and Canada. This is not the first time that Eastern Bloc athletes have defected to the West in search of a better life and more opportunities to compete internationally. Details of this development, that has rocked the tennis world today, will be covered in anther exclusive article by this humble reporter in tomorrow's news.

Chapter 25: Loose Ends

Travis was on a sabbatical recovering from the attack on his life in Hamburg. The event had left a scar on his neck on one side and he had taken to wearing neckties, ascots and turtlenecks. The two young tennis stars had made a quick and smooth transition and had become much sought after for interviews by sports media as well as political talk shows. One had settled in the US and the other had found a home in Canada.

The murderous attacks on Tango Section operatives had ceased and they had started the process of recruiting and training replacements. That had been one of the bright spots in his hospital recovery. Travis had still been in the hospital when the paperwork package for a recently retired USAF Major Stanley White, who last served at Incirlik Air Base in Turkey. It seems Maj. White had asked Travis for a recommendation. He got the recommendation and was in the training system now.

Travis had made a leisurely drive down to the

Costa Bravo area of Spain and returned the equipment that Carlos Bissell had loaned him and then fitted his own AK-47 into the trunk lid. Carlos had been more than helpful in the little project as he and Travis chatted. Travis had caught Carlos looking at his neck more than once but the retired SAS man only asked one question, "Travis, are you OK?"

"Carlos, I have never been better!" Travis responded and gave him a smile that went all the way to his eyes. Carlos just smiled, slapped Travis on the back and did not ask any more questions.

On the other hand Maria had a million questions. Travis managed to explain away the scar on his neck as a freak accident while he was helping the authorities deal with the fellow who had tried to shoot Julie. He finally got her attention off of his injury by asking questions about the business.

He finally got her whole attention when he asked her to take over fulltime management of the company. She jumped up and hugged him when he got to the part of the deal that offered her a way to buy into part ownership. It was clearly a moment of mixed feeling for her, since he was planning to move to Italy.

The group from his villa on New Year's Eve got together and Travis had a leisurely lunch with them. He told them the same fiction about his freak accident and that the authorities had taken care of the fellow who tried to kill Julie. But when they asked when Julie might return and what his plans were, he told them that next year's New Years Eve party would be a place they had not yet found in Italy, probably Naples.

The ladies were particularly distressed by this news but their attitudes began to change when Travis assured them there would be frequent travel between Italy and Spain. And he swore them to secrecy that he fully planned to drive next to a country estate outside of London where Julie was with her sister, Meredith. And when he arrived he planned to ask her to marry him. Then he pulled out the ring box that was burning a hole in his pocket and opened it to get the ladies' approval. In the next moments there were a few tears, then smiles and many handshakes and pats on the back from the men present.

That had been two days ago and he was passing

through Frankfurt again so he could stop and say goodbye to Ervin and his family. They were headed to the United States where he had arranged to buy a small taxi company in Oklahoma City. The business, which he knew well, came thanks to the "reward" he had been given by the US Government for his service. As to where he and his family had chosen to resettle, his wife's cousin was living there and it seemed a good fit for them.

Travis thanked Ervin and told his wife and daughter how brave and intelligent he had been in bringing Farouq to justice. They shared with Travis that they had heard much the same thing from the German Officer who had helped with their initial entry into Germany. Hans Feldman had come by the day before.

When Travis left them he made a call to Hans and then drove to his home and rang the bell. Hans came out to answer the door and the two had a quiet evening over a couple of beers. Travis crashed in the apartment one more night and left before dawn to head to England.

Last Few Miles

And now Travis had crossed the channel on unpaid leave for an unspecified period of time to rest, recover and relocate to Italy. In the never-ending cycle of re-organizations of Tango Section the operational HQ was being relocated to Rome from Madrid. Sheila Makinley had taken over as the acting Head of Operations with the "old man's" retirement. Travis had sent word to her that he wasn't sure he wanted to return to operations.

Sheila had responded that as the acting Tango Alpha, she felt he "owed" her for all the messes she had to clean up behind him all these years. Then more seriously she added that he could name his terms because the organization likely would not have survived without that last operation. "Besides," she had said, "Putin is still out there somewhere and we can't get to him yet. We definitely need your skills. Hell, we would not have even found him without your instincts."

Travis had ended the session by showing Sheila the ring and telling her, "Let's see if Julie says 'yes' and if she does, what she has to say about the whole thing. I still have to convince her to leave the airlines and move to Italy." That had brought a knowing smile from Sheila who only said, "Then get out of here and get busy. You have a big job ahead of you and I have work to do to make this re-org and relocation work."

That had been after the time in Alicante with old friends and before the stop in Germany. Now he was driving on the wrong side of the road in the land of warm beer, bland cuisine, and questionable weather. "What do the Brits see in this place anyway?" Travis asked the dashboard as he drove along. He found the way to the country estate in the early afternoon.

As he crossed a little stone bridge over which the old jaguar barely fit, and rounded a blind curve, he was confronted by two very fit looking men outfitted as hunters. They both were complete with shotguns cradled in their arms and wicker baskets, for birds they might have killed. All of this was quite prominent in the back of their Land Rover that appeared to be casually blocking his way. One of them stepped forward and asked, "Are ye lost, man?"

"No, I don't think so." Travis responded.

They looked at each other and then the other one said, "Yank are you?"

"Yes, I am looking for someone who lives out this way, I think. Her name is Julie and her sister is named Meredith." Travis said immediately.

"And what is your name, sir?" The first man asked.

"My name is Charles Travis Lemon. And I believe their male relative is a retired Brigadier." Travis replied.

"Well, at least ye have good taste in cars." The first man said and then turned to his companion. "Move the Land Rover, Stanfield, and I will ride the rest of the way with Mister Lemon here, that is if he doesn't mind."

"Not at all." Travis said as he reached across to open the jaguar's door. The fellow got in and the two of them rode in silence up to a huge two-story stone country house that looked as though it had always been here.

As they pulled to a stop the front door opened and the passenger said, "Stanfield called ahead." But he got no further as Julie came running out of the front door with Meredith in tow. Travis had barely gotten out of the car when Julie literally jumped into his arms. The passenger spoke again, but this time he turned to Meredith, "Well I guess we let the right one through then."

Meredith ignored the attempt at humor and as Travis set Julie down she came up to him and said simply, "Well."

Travis dropped to one knee reaching into is pants pocket and came out with the little black velvet covered box. He opened it with both hands and said simply, "Julie, would you please do me the honor of being my wife?"

Julie laughed and cried and said yes a dozen times. When things settled down everyone was smiling and Meredith looked over at the hunter who had ridden with Travis, "Yes, you definitely let the right one through!"

Then she turned to Travis and said through her own smile, "Good move there yank, otherwise would have had to shoot you." Then she hugged the two of them. It was clear that Julie was happy and Meredith was smiling and laughing. Even the fellow holding the shotgun was smiling.

Travis could not have imagined a better end to this day.

Thanks for sharing your time with me,
I sincerely hope you enjoyed the story.
~*Mitch Bouchette*

mitchbouchette@gmail.com

Mitch Bouchette is quite a remarkable and versatile writer who publishes in multiple genres. He has a keen wit and a lifetime of travel experience that lends an air of authenticity to his work. Besides, he may be the first Redneck, Hispanic-Cajun you have ever run across. His stories will grab your head and your heart as the characters come alive on the page.

If you enjoy romance novels, please take a look:

THE SMELL OF RAIN: A Romance As It Should Be: Mitch brings you into a world of the beauty of love off the beaten path, on the island of Eleuthra, Bahamas – in his favorite getaway – The Pink Sand Cottage. This place is magical and the stories will touch your heart as the vignettes unfold, tempestuous and sometimes sad, and he will touch your heart as only he can. Have a glass of wine and enjoy!

FEEL THE RAIN: A Romance Rekindled As It Should Be: Mitch Bouchette takes us to Topsail Island, NC where Sara Brown, a successful lawyer from Virginia who is coming off of a messy divorce. She returns to Topsail where she grew up as a girl to find herself and recover control of her life. What she finds is her High School sweetheart, himself a widower, who has deep feelings for her. The appearance of her Ex-husband complicates things as the roller coaster that is her life picks up speed.

AFTER THE RAIN: Love In The Time Of COVID: Mitch introduces us to Thad and Molly who are both headed to the same house on the Outer Banks. Molly and her kids are headed to the OBX to join her BFF from college for a three-week holiday. Thad, her BFF's divorced older brother is headed there early to prep for a family gathering and he is not on board with Molly and her kids joining the family vacation. Then the bridges are closed due to COVID and they are thrown together for three weeks and things get interesting.

On the other hand if you enjoy a bit more action, please check out these titles.

THE SWORD OF RULE: Newen and Izel: What if I told you a story of Vikings raiding in Central America? Mitch Bouchette tells a tale of conquest, treason and love as only he can! The action adventure and romance pulls the reader into the lives of three couples separated by thousands of miles and thousands of years. The story will capture your imagination as the modern day Museum Director connects with her boyfriend's discoveries on a glacier 2000 years later with the conflict between Newen from Yokot'an and the Viking Aenar.

GAELIN'S RAID: Sword Of Rule Viking Series (Book 2): Mitch pulls the reader into a world of adventure, conquest and action. This is the story of Irish Vikings and explorers whose lives intertwine across the centuries. The result is a linkage of civilizations of different peoples and different cultures that developed on different continents. It ties them together across different ages from 850 AD to modern times in a heart warming and sometimes explosive story.

And if you might enjoy an irreverent and unlikely peek into "coming of age" of young men educated at The Citadel these might suit your taste.

SOUTHERN RULES (Book 1): If you grew up in the 60s, Vietnam was more than a name on a map and Civil Rights was more than just a history lesson. Southern Rules is the story of young men attending The Citadel and learning to deal with the realities of that era – from first loves to race confrontations to preparing for service in Vietnam and the Hippie counter-culture. The story will make you laugh and perhaps cry on occasion but you will identify with the characters and the crazy world they experienced.

MORE SOUTHERN RULES (BOOK 2): is a work of fiction involving the same improbable characters of the 1960s and 1970s coming together in Vietnam and Germany. The story of these young military officers comes to life against historically accurate events. If you are a child of the 60s and 70s then the Vietnam War, the Civil Rights Movement, terrorism in Germany and the craziness that made up your world is more than just a place on a map or a history lesson. This book is written for YOU so sit back and enjoy the story to relive your memories of the era.

And the first book in this series.

TANGO SECTION OPERATIVE #5 (BOOK 1) RESCUE FROM IRAN: In 1979 the world is in a special kind of turmoil with tensions in the Middle East,

Germany is divided East and West, and the Soviet Union USSR is alive and well. Tango Section is an obscure group of operatives who are sent to work specific high interest cases . . . any way the can! Meet Charles Travis Lemon; Tango Section Operative Five – Tango 5.

Made in the USA
Middletown, DE
01 March 2023